ABRACADABRA

THE DRAGON STORM

ANTHONY DIPAOLO

Written and Printed in the United States of America

For more information, or to book an event, contact
ADiPaolo@TheDragonStorm.com

Special Thanks to Michelle DiPaolo, your love and support makes this possible; Thank you to Josh Horowitz & Gunner Lindbloom - your friendships & assistance have been invaluable.

Book Design and Layout: Anthony DiPaolo
Cover Design and Concept Designs: Anthony DiPaolo

Copy Edited by
Josh Horowitz

ISBN 979-8-9894841-0-2
First US Paperback Edition

~

Through the gates of Heaven
to the altars of Hell
The power is at my command...
Yngwie J. Malmsteen

~

~

For My Two Sons,
Anthony Domenick and Thomas Alexander.
The True Magic in My Life.

~

BOOK I

1

"Abracadabra!"

The obsidian-shrouded magician stirred about the small stage. The prestidigitator's arms spun and flexed as he whirled a rather large black and red linen sheet about.

"Abracadabra!"

Alexander Storm sat motionless in the back row of a small Parisian theater, his eyes transfixed on the movements of the entertainer. The sheet. His hands. His eyes. All actions tirelessly choreographed to achieve obfuscation and stylized confusion in the senses of the beholder. The dimly lit venue buzzed with stale smoke and bourbon, intermingled with the musky aroma of teak oil. A thick haze, comprised of patrons' cigars and cigarettes, as well as some measure of theatrically introduced smoke, hung in the air slightly above stage level. Alexander's mind wandered absently to the dense morning miasma of the Japanese fukaki kiri matō - the impenetrable clusters of ghostlike clouds that often descend on the Oriental forests in August.

"What is a word?" the illusionist pondered aloud, his movements clearly captivating his small seat-filled audience of no more than fifty spectators, "A sound? An orator's thoughts made real... brought to life?"

Storm allowed his eyes to wander away from the stage as he studied the faces of the men and women in the rows between the performer's perch and himself. They too were focused on the magician, their thrill-seeking appetites waiting to devour the otherworldly display that was promised by the friends and family who had come before them.

"Presto!" the slender mystic shouted through permanently grinning lips.

Some of the observers jumped, and a woman towards the front cried out ever so slightly. Alexander employed his finely tuned ears, absorbing the magician's words while searching for the roots of his origins. He was most certainly not a native, evidenced by both the nature and unrefined tone of his accent. His was not the voice of a romantic.

Hungarian, perhaps? Storm felt his assessment weak due to the scarcity of samples provided by the performer.

"When we utter a word," said the performer, pausing all movement for effect, "does the sound stop at the listener's ears... or does it travel on and beyond... for eternity?"

Alexander watched as the illusionist tossed a large square of fabric to the stage floor and took a step back. The slightly matted material landed perfectly upon the tattered wood floor below. There was no crease nor wrinkle evident in the linen, as if it had been laid and flattened by hand, though it had not.

"*Pulchritudo!*" the magician whispered with force, extending his arms.

The audience gasped as he lifted his arms upward, causing the sheet to rise. Alexander shifted slightly in his seat and allowed a faint smirk to creep across his lips. The linen grew about five feet in the air, taking on the distinctive shape of a human form. Moving forward, the conjurer took a firm hold of the sheet and yanked it to his side, revealing a woman below.

Patrons of the small theater came to life, cheering and clapping at what was obviously a display of authentic magic. The magician's assistant, scantily clad in tight black leather, bowed to the audience. Alexander took note of her Asian origins, as well as the wide array of tattoos that covered the many visible portions of her body. Most notably, he eyed the ritualistically accurate pentagram encircling her belly button.

As the applause began to die down, several members of the male audience whistled and bellowed with over-exaggerated cat calls.

The magician smiled. "Careful my fine gentlemen," he remarked, "she is a man killer."

Although the performance was well-orchestrated for such a trivial, antiquated location, Alexander was quite confident that Atticus the Great was nothing more than an imaginative carpenter, making good use of trapdoors and sliding panels.

"I sense we still have some who do not believe in the power of the word," said Atticus, shaking his head dramatically at his assistant, who placed her hands on her hips and winked at the crowd. "Let us see if we may not sway the direction of our non-believers."

The magician turned and stared directly at Alexander. The thick band of black makeup encircling the performer's eyes created the illusion of a phantasmal glow. Alexander leaned forward in his rickety theater seat, never breaking the connection that Atticus had established.

"Very well!" Atticus shouted, and he waved his hand, causing the linen that had dropped to the stage floor at his side to crawl and expand flat again between himself and the assistant. "Shall we?"

"Leo!" Atticus cried out, his eyes still locked upon Alexander. This time it was the leather-bound assistant who lifted her hands to the heavens. The sheet reacted by expanding, first by stretching out to almost triple its size, then up into a large, indiscernible form.

Alexander Storm's heart began to pound in his chest like an abhorrent child at play as a mighty roar filled the diminutive theater. He watched as the magician's audience pressed back in their seats and gasped at the reveal. As Atticus swiped the sheet away, a massive lion roared with such force that its head wobbled back and forth uncontrollably.

"Nice kitty," said Atticus the Great, as he smiled and tossed the sheet back over the beast's head. "Good kitty..."

"Alakazam!"

Storm sprang to his feet as the lion vanished beneath the linen, which lay flush once more.

"Doubting Thomas... doubting Thomas," Atticus said, as he

began to pace the stage around the sheet. "What can I do to eradicate your disbelief?"

Alexander was quite sure he was being addressed directly. He watched as some members of the audience scurried past him to the exit, causing the heavy mist permeating the air to part and swirl around him.

"I've got it!" Atticus exclaimed, paying no heed to his fleeing spectators.

Alexander moved through his row and stepped out into the center aisle which divided the old theater's seating.

"DRACO!"

The magician's sheet rose up to the ceiling of the auditorium and Alex reached out to steady himself on the back of the nearest seat. Onlookers were fleeing and screaming now as they pushed their way towards the exit. The unexpected exodus of the audience caused Storm to step into the row to his left to avoid being trampled. He watched in awe as a fiery inferno engulfed the sheet and exposed a colossal dragon beneath.

Roaring with hissing fury, the reptilian myth spread its wings and released another fireball into the open air. Alexander caught sight of Atticus and his assistant to the rear of the dragon, opposite each other. He watched as they bent down and took hold of the corner of what appeared to be the stage curtain, tossing it up and over the dragon in a supernatural display of control.

"PRESTO!"

No sooner had the words left Atticus' mouth, than the creature dematerialized beneath the heavy curtain, causing it to drop to the stage with an audible thud.

Alexander, still disoriented by the display, struggled to make his way back into the aisle before beginning to move towards the stage.

"And that my friends," said Atticus, as he and his assistant quickly moved in front of the curtain at their feet, "concludes this evening's lessons."

"Who are you?" Storm demanded, approaching the first row of seats.

Atticus' head snapped in the direction of his approach and Storm froze at the sight of his fiery pupils.

"One last trick, master?" said the assistant, whose English was tattered by her Asian accent.

"Oh, very well," replied Atticus.

"I demand your name," said Alexander, who was on the move again, approaching the wall of the stage.

Laughter echoed off the walls of the now empty theater.

"DAEMONIUM!"

Alexander hoisted himself up onto the stage and sprang to his feet. It was too late. A massive hulk had grown beneath the frayed stage curtain and Alexander threw his body backward instinctively, landing hard on the first row of seats below. Fighting through the stinging pain of his muscles and bones, he righted himself just in time to watch Atticus and his assistant lift the front of the curtain, exposing, for just a split second, the abomination beneath.

Asmodeus!

Storm recognized the beast beneath the curtain. Mired in revelation, he watched as Atticus the Great and his companion stepped under the towering curtain. Lurching forward, Alexander once more took to scaling the stage wall and clambered to his feet.

His efforts were unrewarded, however, as a single word escaped from beneath the sprawling curtain to his ears, and with it, the figures beneath vanished.

"ABRACADABRA!"

2

The morning light crept through the arched stone windows of Kate's bedroom and tickled the nerves of her cheek with its heat. Yawning, she extended her arms in a v-stretch and opened her eyes to greet the new day. Every day, it seemed, was a *new* day at Dragon Loch. Some novel adventure was always just around the corner, waiting for her to delve into. The research and investigation lab Alexander had designed for her was the stuff of dreams. The field work, when Storm felt inclined to include her, offered satisfaction like she had never experienced before. She was happy.

Kate quickly showered, dressed, and made her way down to the great hall that had become one of her favorite locations in the castle. Over the last eighteen months she had spent many an hour engaged in long conversations covering every topic imaginable in the picturesque castle dining hall. Along with Keith and Abigail, she was enjoying fine libations and gourmet delights, often until the wee hours of the morning, and they had marveled at their benefactor's tales of high adventure and exploration. After the events that had culminated in the sands of Egypt a year-and-a-half before, the three companions had decided to take Storm up on his offer to stay on at Dragon Loch... indefinitely. Sadly, Samantha had decided to return to her cyber-empire of technology and relative seclusion. Kate spoke and texted with her often, and she was confident that one day Sam would return to them, completing the "storm," as Alexander referred to it on more than one occasion.

The huge wooden double doors of the hall swung in, revealing Philip waiting for her arrival within.

"Good morning, Miss Kate," said the elderly jack-of-all-things-castle. He flashed her a quick smile, which Kate was pretty sure he reserved for her alone, before stepping to one side.

"Good morning," she replied, making her way to the lengthy carved wooden banquet table.

"Allow me, Miss Kate," said Philip, as he trotted past her and withdrew the tall-backed antique chair at the head of the table. Nodding, she quickly sat and allowed him to push her in, flip out her linen napkin, and place it on her lap.

"Why, thank you, Philip."

Kate smiled at the pomp that the old-timer clearly enjoyed, or so she surmised, as it had become a morning ritual for them. The entire idea of being treated in such a manner had taken some getting used to, and there were many weeks of uncontrollable giggling between her and Abigail.

"I have prepared a delightful start to your day, my dear."

Philip had the uncanny ability to present her, especially at breakfast, with exactly what she was in the mood for without ever inquiring. The uncomfortableness this created in the beginning was quickly replaced by appreciation. Kate nodded with gratitude, never doubting for a moment that she was about to be offered that which she desired.

Philip began to shuffle towards the kitchen entrance when Kate called out after him, "Will Alexander be joining me, Philip?"

The caretaker stopped and turned back to her, tapping his forehead with the palm of his hand. "Almost forgot," he repeated several times. "Damn senility."

"Like a fox," Kate retorted.

Philip perked up at her compliment. "A silver fox, perhaps," he joked, and withdrew an envelope from the inner pocket of his gold-trimmed smoking jacket.

Kate winked. "All the same,"

Philip laughed. "Yes, yes... very good," he murmured, and presented her with the envelope.

Kate took the letter and looked back at Philip, seeking an explanation.

"From Master Storm," Philip said, his expression growing official. "He was called away on business."

"Oh," Kate whispered, with a notable degree of disappointment. Keith had left yesterday, off on some errand in Marrakesh with Asar, while Abigail was still a few days away from returning from a two week visit back home. Kate had been looking forward to some one-on-one time with Alex. Then her growing melancholy was swiftly replaced by excited stomach butterflies. It was hers. All hers. She had the run of Dragon Loch.

A slight smile spread across her face. "I see."

"We will be fine, Miss Kate," Philip assured her.

"Of course," Kate said, allowing her smile to shine through. She would spend the day reading and exploring the castle, and all the while, Philip would care for her as if she were royalty. Good deal. "We'll be fine."

She winked at Philip, then turned her attention to the envelope as Philip returned to his slow and steady trek to the stoves.

Inserting her pinky nail under the flap, Kate hastily tore the top open and withdrew the note from within. Unfolding the trifold page, she began to read the precisely drawn characters that comprised the message.

My Dear Kate,

Please forgive my discourteous departure. I have been summoned to the South of France to evaluate the validity of rumors which I suspect will amount to nothing more than tomfoolery and charlatanism in its grandest form. I am, however, obligated to investigate the claims as they have been set forth at the bequest of a reliable individual to whom I am somewhat indebted... so... so be it. Please enjoy the essence of your solitude, as well as the charmed attentions of dear Philip, and I shall return to Dragon Loch in short order.

Fondly yours,

Alexander Storm

P.S. I should note that your solitude shall be only

momentary, as Serket has advised me of her intentions to pay a visit, and perhaps a prolonged one at that, beginning tomorrow's eve. Until I return - A.S.

"Damn," muttered Kate. She dropped the note to the hard-grained surface of the table and shifted herself back against the burgundy cushion that supported her back.

"What's that, Miss Kate?"

Philip had stealthily re-entered the hall and began to approach Kate, balancing a large white porcelain plate in one hand and a polished silver carafe in the other. His free pinky was looped through the handle of a large earthen-colored mug, which dangled and tapped the coffee pot gently as he stepped.

"Oh, nothing really," she replied. "Serket will be joining us tomorrow night."

"Of this, I am aware, Miss Kate," he informed her, as he set the plate and other items down on the tabletop. "You are not fond of our Egyptian friend?"

"No... no," Kate quickly interjected. "I love Serket, Philip... it's not that."

"Three eggs, over-easy... rye toast... crispy, hickory-smoked bacon," said Philip, pausing for effect. "And freshly-ground Turkish coffee... French-pressed, of course. Shall I pour?"

Kate laughed. "Of course... always perfect. Exactly what I would have ordered."

Philip smiled deeply. "My pleasure, Miss Kate... as always."

He set the carafe down on the table and positioned the mug of coffee beside her plate.

"Enjoy your breakfast my dear," he said, as he turned to leave her to it. "Pay no mind to the dishes - I shall return for them in short order."

"Thanks." Kate barely got the words out from behind her mouthful of eggs. She had no time to waste. There was a castle to explore.

3

Alexander knelt down and took the edge of the tattered and frayed curtain in his hands. Tugging with some degree of force, he lifted the ornately embellished material up and folded it over on itself, almost in half, exposing the scorched wood beneath. Retrieving his cell phone from his pocket, Alex tapped the flashlight on, illuminating the dark surface of the stage below. There was something there within the burn patterns that the magician had left behind. Dragging the surprisingly heavy curtain to one side, Storm exposed the entirety of the lines and curves that Atticus' magic display had presumably created.

"Lessons..." he mused, recalling the assistant's inquiry to her master during the show. "And to what teachings did she refer, I wonder?"

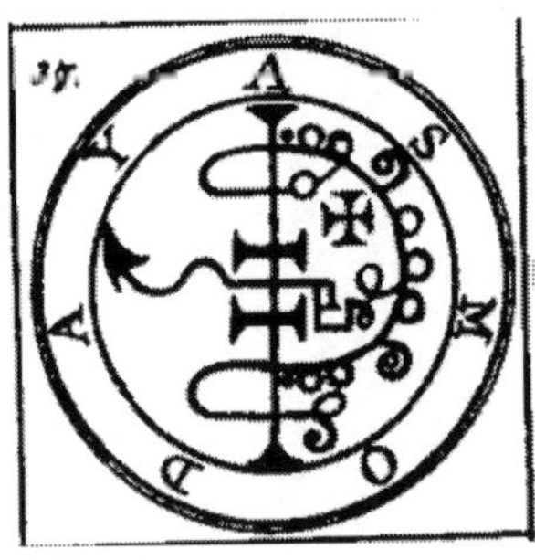

The ashen symbol he had exposed spoke volumes to that end, and confirmed his suspicions that Atticus, whoever the hell he was, had taken to communing with demons to achieve his awe-inspiring magical feats.

THE SYMBOL WAS KNOWN as a sigil - a unique seal that acted as both an identifier and a ritualistic summoning mark. Alex was well acquainted with whom this particular sigil belonged. Having extensively studied the *Dictionnaire Infernal*, J Collin de Plancy's 1818 compendium of all things demonic, he was familiar with the majority of the symbols and seals representing the forces of chaos and darkness. It was no surprise to Storm that the mark left behind was that of Asmodeus, a king of Hell and commander of 72 legions of the damned. Alex had been fairly confident that he had properly identified the beast earlier, even though he had only been afforded a brief glimpse beneath the curtain, and now the sigil confirmed his fears.

"A conundrum..." Alex mused, the words barely leaving his lips as he took several shots of the branded stage with his cell phone. "Some madness is clearly afoot."

Storm's thoughts were cut short by the faint rustling sounds that were emanating from the wings upstage. Spinning to meet the noise, Alex trained his light on the darkness and watched for any signs of movement. Nothing.

Averting the beam of light to the floor at his feet, Alex stood there several minutes peering into the indiscernible darkness beyond.

Darkness possesses the ability to take on a life of its own when one stares into it long enough. The human eye, it would seem, attempts to create light where there is none. Our subconscious remains instinctively fearful of the deep void of pitch black, and compensates for the absence of illumination by sending false impulses of floating spots and shimmering shadows to the brain.

Registering no movement at points beyond, Alex turned his attentions back to the symbol at his feet. Bending down, he ran his fingers over the lines and curves of the mark and was shocked to find that the sigil was formed by a raised relief in the wooden stage. He had erroneously expected the symbol to have been created by the task of carving or scorching, but this was something entirely different.

Rising, he circled around the shape and took several more photographs.

BANG!

Someone, or something, had slammed the stage with great force in the wings to his right, and Alex jumped in reply. Shinning his light in the general direction of the silence-breaking thud, Alex walked forward, following the beam of light towards the rear of the small theater.

HEHEHEHEHEH

The faint, echoing sounds of child-like laughter rang out behind Alex, and he spun around to face the seats of the empty hall.

"Who's there?" he demanded. "Show yourself!"

HEHEHEHEH

This time the eerie laughter originated from the darkness of the wings.

"By that sin fell the angels," Storm whispered, recalling a line of apropos Shakespeare for comfort.

Turning about once more to face the rear of the theater, Alex searched for the source of the malevolent laughter that was now coming in sporadic barrages from all sides.

Alexander was spinning about as the spine-chilling resonances flew at him. His eyes found the exit on the opposite side of the theater and his thoughts quickly embraced the idea of the cool, silent night air beyond the door. Committing to this goal, and his ultimate quest to be free of the intensifying assault on his sanity, Alex took a step towards the edge of the wooden stage. It was then that his peripheral vision registered an approaching mass from beyond the wings, freezing Alexander Storm where he stood.

4

"Relax, son," Asar said, smiling at Keith reassuringly as he lifted the glass mug of mint tea to his lips. "Morocco is quite peaceful… I promise."

Keith nodded to his companion half-heartedly and gazed through the door back into the Kasbah du Toubkal hotel and restaurant. The classic Moroccan design and bright inviting colors, eclectically tossed together as they were, did offer an air of tranquility.

"Look," Asar offered with a bear-like growl. "Look upon that, my friend."

Keith followed his gesture to the majestic canopy of snow-capped mountains lining the backdrop of the establishment. From their seats on the stilted patio of Kasbah du Toubkal, the view of the Atlas Mountains was, at the very least, awe inspiring, and Keith drew a deep breath of crisp air into his lungs.

"That's the spirit." Asar took another gulp of warm tea. "Drink," he prodded, to which Keith complied.

"Not bad," Keith said, smiling as he returned the cup for another swig.

Asar's brow drew tight in insult, as if he had grown and picked the leaves that made up the ancient brew himself. "Not bad? It is marvelous!"

Keith laughed. "That's what I meant."

Asar's face returned to a state of serenity, the paternal warmth setting Keith at ease. He turned once more and looked upon the grandeur of the mountainous landscape.

"You sure those aren't the Himalayas?" Keith asked in a tone tantamount to sarcasm.

"Atlas," Asar replied curtly, the inflection of his travel companion's words sailing right above his large Egyptian head. "They are the Atlas Mountains. The mistake is quite common, young man."

Keith sat up in his ornately designed iron seat as the waiter emerged from the inner dining area with a platter of food carefully balanced on one palm.

"Ahhh," Asar laughed, "you have drunk like a Moroccan." The waiter placed two bowls in front of each of them. "Now you will know what it is like to eat in the shadow of the Atlas."

The local cuisine placed before Keith gave forth an extremely pleasing aroma. He leaned into the mist of heat radiating from the colorful dishes and indulged his senses a bit deeper.

"This is mouthwatering lamb tangia, my boy," Asar instructed, pointing to the stew-like dish in front of them. "And this is a fragrant couscous. You may mix them together if you so wish," he added, pointing at the dish that accompanied it.

Without further words, Asar began to greedily savor the tangia, which he accompanied with heaping portions of the couscous.

"Ummm..." Keith laughed. The big guy was in heaven.

Asar smiled, signaling to Keith's bowels, "Eat. Then you too will know nirvana."

Keith took a mouthful of the couscous first, allowing the unsuspecting flavors to dance around his mouth. He swallowed and smirked at Asar.

"Oh yeah... I got you, big guy,"

Keith quickly delved into the lamb with equal signs of satisfaction.

The two men sat there in silence, nodding at each other. They were enjoying the food, the view, and peculiarly enough, each other's oddly paired company.

Keith, finally breaking from his stomach's onslaught of food intake, seized a sip of his tea and sat back. "So... what are we here for?" he began.

Asar looked at him and hurried to chew and swallow what was in his mouth.

"Not that I mind," Keith added, waving his hand about at the impressive scene around them. "Not minding this at all."

"We are here," Asar started, wiping the residual sauce from his thick beard, "for... that."

Asar smiled at someone behind Keith and rose from his seat. Quickly spying the man reading a paper alone at the table next to them, he placed his paw-like hand on the seat's back and nodded to the gentleman, who raised his head in agreement. Asar spun around with the chair and slid it to the table near him and Keith. Their visitor came into Keith's view at the same moment, and he too jumped to his feet and nodded slightly as the tall, exotic-complexioned woman allowed her body to gingerly fall into the extra seat. Asar reclaimed his seat and signaled for Keith to do the same.

Asar took the woman's dark-skinned hand gently in his and smiled. "May I introduce Zorha," he said. "This is Keith."

The woman turned momentarily to Keith, barely casting him a

glance from beneath her absurdly large black sunglasses. The smile she offered was even slimmer.

"How are you, my dear?" Asar inquired.

"Fine," Zorha nervously replied, standing momentarily to swing her swank designer backpack off her body, which was adorned in a long, rather snug, red dress and black heels that were higher than the dress was tight. Keith quickly surmised that the woman's wardrobe was probably worth more than he earned in an entire year.

"Take it," her voice cracked, as she shoved the bag under the table towards Asar. "Just take the whole bag."

"Woah there," Asar responded with the palm of his hand. "I do not think it matches my ensemble, Zorha... please relax."

"Relax," she snapped back, withdrawing the bag and dropping it at her black heels. "Have you any idea what I had to go through to get this... this... thing?"

"I do not," said Asar, his voice complex now, and the serious nature of his tone smacked Keith with a sobering blast. They were there on business for Alexander Storm. *Why would this be anything but a grave task?* Keith thought. *Perhaps life or death... apocalyptic even... all of the above... take your pick.*

"Tell your master I am done," Zorha said, attempting to rise from her seat.

"Sit," Asar commanded. Their guest stared at him a moment before eventually submitting.

"It's in a pouch," she offered. "In the bag."

"Take it out and hand it to me, if you will."

"Out in the open?"

"It is a pouch," Asar replied, his voice even and in control. "Nothing more... unless you make it something more. So let us part ways with the theatrics, shall we?"

Zorha huffed and lifted the backpack into her lap. Undoing the pull strap that cinched the top closed, she reached in and produced a small velvet satchel and placed it on the table.

Asar nodded and picked the bag up. He did not rush to secret it away, but instead rolled his fingers around the outside tracing the bumps and nubs that comprised the object within.

"Very good," said Asar. He smiled, his tone jovial again, and placed the object Zorha had delivered into the inner pocket of his jacket. "Would you care for some tea? Waiter..."

"No," she snapped, rising from her seat. "Now tell Storm I am done... debt paid... got it?"

Asar shook his head. "Sit down."

Once again, she paused momentarily as if to feign some degree of rebellion, but eventually returned to her seat.

"Zorha," Asar spoke softly, "I do not believe your debt to Mr. Storm is paid." He paused. "But that is for him to say, not I... and certainly not you."

"But..." she started.

"But," he mimicked, "I am sure he will be extremely grateful for your assistance in this regard." Asar tapped the concealed object. "And he will respond to your inquiry, which I shall politely convey, in the like."

Zorha nodded in agreement. "Just let him know that grave robbing from the forbidden grounds of the Saadian Tombs was not what I signed up for... 'kay?"

Asar nodded as the waiter arrived. "Another tea if you will, sir," said the server.

Zorha stood up once more. "No, I'm not staying."

The waiter nodded and departed from what he correctly appraised as a potentially volatile interaction in the making.

"Please," Asar implored. "Stay."

"No thank you," she said, swinging her pack onto her back. "I'm glad to be rid of it... I've had horrible nightmares, even while I'm wide awake, since I procured it."

"Well, that's not really a nightmare then," Keith absently interjected. "If you're not asleep, then..."

"Shut up!" she shouted at Keith who recoiled in visible fear of the woman's building wrath.

"Zorha!" Asar chided.

"No," she said, turning. "No more. Good luck with that."

Keith watched as she marched away, her heels clicking on the classically decorated tiles beneath her fury. Turning sharply at the entrance back into the restaurant's dining room, she practically knocked a young waiter to the ground as he stood vigil in the wings, before she disappeared into the darkened ambiance of the room and was gone.

"Lovely girl," Asar remarked wryly, returning to his meal. "Always a pleasure."

5

Silence filled the small theater, and Alexander was thankful. The cacophony of whispers, laughter and unearthly murmurs suddenly ceased all at once upon the arrival of the figure moving across the stage. Alex's body remained motionless as his eyes traced the path of the stout older man to the back of the stage. Allowing the muscles of his neck to twist ever so slightly, he kept the mysterious individual in his view and watched as he took some unseen steps in the wing and slowly disappeared in his descent offstage.

With the stealthy movements of a wolf on the hunt, Storm swiveled to the left on the tips of his toes and took to following the spectral figure into the darkness of the curtain-shrouded recesses of the theater. Alexander took a moment to shine the light of his cell ahead into the beckoning gloom, illuminating the steps at the edge of the stage. He could make out the outlines of a walkway or hall, and what appeared to be several framed doorways along the route. He found no traces of the old man, nor indications of the path his quarry had taken after exiting the stage.

Storm swapped hands to hold the phone in his left hand, lowering it to hip level. In an effortless motion one could surmise had been rehearsed ad-infinitum, he silently snapped his right wrist and squeezed his fist around the handle of a long blade that appeared from beneath his sleeve. Without further hesitation, he descended the steps in pursuit of what appeared to be the only remaining inhabitant of the deserted theater.

Placing his cell upright in the semi-open palm of his right hand, Storm allowed its base edge to rest securely on the handle of the blade and attempted the knobs of the doors he passed with his left. After testing the locks on five doors unsuccessfully, he arrived at a sixth and final door. Turning the handle, he expected to be met with the same degree of resistance as the others, but was instead caught at a disadvantage when the door creaked open before he could pull it back.

Retrieving his light source from his right hand, Alexander shone the beam of light into the entranceway and slammed the bottom of his heavy shoe into the door, driving it wide open with a shuddering blast. Springing forward, with his shimmering silver blade retracted and ready for a thrusting strike should it become necessary, he plunged into the unknown.

Taking inventory of his surroundings with the speed of a viper, he surmised he had entered the makeshift living quarters of a property master or the like. There was a single bed in disarray, a dresser with a mix of toiletries and a sparse few pictures and mementos atop, a rickety wooden chair near a single serving table in one corner, and the back of the shadowy old man, head oddly bowed, in the other.

Alexander's mind registered and reacted to the eerie picture that was painted before him. Turning his body slightly in the figure's direction, Alex readied his weapon and advanced towards the occupied corner of the room.

"Who are you?" Storm demanded. "Show yourself."

A low moan answered Alexander's inquiry, and he felt the fine hairs that traversed his neck rise in response.

"What are you doing here?" demanded Storm. He gave no indication of fear and resumed his forward advance. The darkness behind him replied to the continuing moans and took to resuming the bloodcurdling laughter that had previously brought victims to the edge of madness.

Alex blinked his eyes rapidly as he employed ancient techniques of relaxation and focus to blot out the spell-ridden laughter that once again was echoing through the theater.

"Speak... I demand it! Explain yourself... where is Atticus?"

The figure visibly reacted to the utterance of the magician's name and slowly turned to face his inquisitor. Storm was shocked to find a meek, older gentleman, clothed in a finely fitted usher's uniform. His face smiled timidly at him.

"English?" Alex asked, lowering the beam of the intense light slightly from the direction of the usher's squinting eyes. Allowing his blade hand to drop to his side, he used the outer edge of his upper thigh to secret it from the old man's view.

"Do you speak English?" Alex repeated.

"Yes," the old man replied. "What do you want?"

Alexander noted that the demonic laughter had ceased once again, and he moved sideways to the center of the room.

"Atticus," offered Storm, studying the man's expression for signs of recognition, and finding none.

"Who?"

"The magician... who performed tonight."

"I am afraid," the old timer began.

"Atticus the Great," continued Alex, attempting to clarify his request. "The magic show... tonight... he performed to a sold-out house. Surely..."

"Tonight?" the man interrupted.

Alex paused and studied the man. *Was he drunk or daft?* "Tonight," he finally conceded. "He performed tonight."

"Impossible," the old man said, waiving Alex off as he began to cross the room in the direction of the door. His hobbling steps and slight stature was disarming, and Alex rapidly found himself at a disadvantage as the old man stood between him and the room's exit.

"Why is that?" Alex said, intending to keep the conversation afloat, yet sensing the deception before him. He watched as the man turned his back to Alex and took several steps towards the door.

"STOP!" Alex demanded, and the figure complied. "Why is that impossible, old man?"

"Arrête! C'est ici l'empire de la Mort," the spectral figure bellowed out, sending shivers down Alexander's body, as the faint, yet rising, sinister symphony of laughter began again.

"What did you say?!"

Alexander's body grew limp as the figure turned to face him. His clothes were tattered and torn - his face barely clad in skin - the rounded edges of his very near skull visible beneath. Eyes hollow and sunken stared at Alexander through the suddenly heavy, sooty air.

"No one performed here tonight," the skull of a face hissed. "Nor the night before... or the night before... or the night preceding that."

Alex allowed his blade to become visible to the apparition, as he used every ounce of will to block out the cursed attack on his ears by the mounting laughter. He needed to make it past the fiend to the door and get the hell out of the theater. His curiosity had previously taken control when he should have used the opportunity to escape the confines of the hellish venue - he was not about to make the same mistake twice. Moving with force towards the figure, he bobbed in one direction and spun past it in the other, his long jacket flying about like a cape through the acrobatics of his actions. He was now between the decaying figure and the threshold.

"Look around you, foolish infidel," spat the wraith as it turned to face him once again. "This theater burnt to rubble over a century ago... taking its patrons and performers with it."

Alexander shook his head at the fiend's words and blinked his eyes, which slowly focused on the dissolving illusion he had been lost in. Spinning round in dizzying disbelief, Alexander Storm suddenly noticed the open night sky above him. He was standing somewhere in the center of a burnt-out shell of a building. The stink of flame-created-carbon filled the air, radiating from the remnants of blackened timber and soot-stained stone and mortar.

Alexander's arms dropped to his side, and he gasped for air that was becoming laborious in his constricting throat. An illusion, a master illusion - for his benefit no less - had been achieved this night. It was like nothing he had ever experienced before, and he inadvertently took a step backwards.

"C'est ici l'empire de la Mort, Alexander Storm!" the ethereal figure growled, teeth bared, its body fading into mist. "C'est ici l'empire de la Mort..."

Alex lunged towards the fading figure, though it was disappearing along with any hope for explanation. "Here lies..." uttered the wraith, its voice trailing off with the final remains of its vanishing form.

"The Empire of Death," Alexander whispered, completing the creature's mantra. "The Empire of Death."

6

"Wait up," said Keith, doing his best to keep up with a man at least thirty years his senior as the two darted for the rolling train.

"We must make this train Mr. Keith," Asar huffed. "William requires our assistance."

Asar lurched forward and grabbed the tarnished silver bar on the exterior of the train car door. Grasping tightly, he hoisted his hulking frame up and into the threshold.

"Quickly," he shouted to his companion, who was laboring to reach for Asar's outstretched hand. "I will leave you if need be."

No freakin' way, Keith thought, as he pushed the last vestiges of energy into his screaming legs. Springing forward from a crouch, he sailed into the air as Asar's hand slammed shut around his own. With the ease of plucking a weed from wet soil, Asar yanked him up and into the car of the train. Keith, exhausted from his trek, remained on the floor where he landed for several seconds before grabbing hold of the stair rail above.

"That was close," he blurted out, still exasperated but doing his best to disguise his condition.

Asar's hearty laugh filled the train car. "Less Burger King perhaps, young man."

Keith smiled and shook his head in agreement. "More lamb, right?"

"Yes... more lamb."

Asar walked up the steps past him and into the ornately decorated sleeper car. Sensing that his older companion was no longer in eyeshot, Keith allowed himself to gulp in a massive burst of air.

Asar popped his face around the corner of the wall at the top of the steps. "Are you coming?"

"Yup," Keith replied arduously as he righted himself and climbed the steps to join Asar.

"Tickets?"

Asar gazed down at the conductor, who had appeared out of nowhere.

"No."

A look of confusion immediately came across the attendant's face, and he reached towards the radio on his belt.

Asar's arm shot out and held the conductor's hand in place on top of his walkie-talkie. "No need for that, kind sir," he began.

The conductor attempted to struggle with the colossal Egyptian, but to no avail. Asar had his arm pinned against his own hip, and Keith snickered at the comical display of the skirmish.

"Not helpful, Mr. Keith," Asar advised, peering back over his shoulder.

Returning his attention back to the car attendant, he said, "This is car six, is it not?"

"What?"

"Car six, correct?"

"Yes, six."

Asar relinquished his hold on the frightened man and took a step back next to Keith. "Cabin six," Asar continued, and he leaned down and presented the panicked conductor with a small card he had withdrawn from his jacket.

"What?"

Swiping the business card from Asar's hand, the conductor held it up in front of his spectacled face for review. Lowering the card slightly, just enough for Keith to see his eyes, he scrutinized the duo.

"Follow me," he finally instructed. "You could have stated your business up front, you know."

Asar opened his mouth to engage the attendant, but reconsidered and turned to wink at Keith instead, who shrugged in ignorance.

"Cabin six," the conductor announced while extending a retractable keyring from his belt and unlocking the door. Without entering the cabin, he slid the wood paneled door open and stepped back, granting Keith and Asar passage. "My regards to Mr. Storm, if you will."

Asar turned to acknowledge his request, as it was indeed a request.

"Of course," he assured the timid man, "Mr.?"

"Pierpont," said the attendant, perking up at the assurance created by Asar's question. "Richard Pierpont."

"Splendid, Richard Pierpont," bellowed Asar, his jovial tone returning. "Mr. Storm will be advised of your assistance."

"Thank you," said the man, and he turned to depart.

Asar cleared his throat loudly, causing Pierpont to do an about-face and return to the doorway.

"Key please," said Asar with an outstretched hand that beckoned compliance.

Pierpont said nothing as he fumbled with his keyring and handed over the key to the cabin.

"Rest assured," Asar said, smiling, "it shall be returned at the end of our journey." Laughing, he continued, "Now Richard, food and wine for our long journey's start."

"There is a food service attendant who will be happy..."

Asar reached out and grasped Pierpont's shoulder tightly. "I would be more comfortable, that is, Mr. Storm would be most appreciative, if you would attend to our needs... personally."

"As you wish," Pierpont said, bending his knees slightly to drop under the tight grip Asar had set upon him.

"Personally," Asar continued, maintaining his grasp on Pierpont. "As in no one else needs to be made aware of our presence... agreed?"

Asar released his shoulder. "Understood," Pierpont exclaimed, just relieved to be free of the man's massive hand. "I shall return forthwith with libations and fine meats and cheeses... will this be to your liking?"

"Hahah... very much so,"

Asar slid the cabin door closed and spun the lock.

"What was that all about?" asked Keith, who dropped onto the couch on one side of the cabin and put his elbows up on the table that stood between himself and the opposite couch.

"Which part?" Asar replied dryly, falling in across from his companion.

"All of it... any of it?"

Asar said nothing, but instead sat back on the couch and put his hand up under the table. Keith watched Asar's expression as the big man searched, sliding his arm back and forth. His thick eyebrows bounced up and down at Keith as he found what he was looking for. An audible *click* emanated from below the table as laser sharp, glowing red lines shot throughout the cabin. Keith watched in amazement as the entire cabin came to life with symbols and cryptic writing. He marveled as the lights extended throughout the spacious cabin like molten steel being slowly poured into a mold. From the floor to the ceiling, window, and walls, the images appeared all around them. Following the light to the back of the cabin door, Keith watched as a circle, star, and scorpion suddenly became evident on the entry barrier.

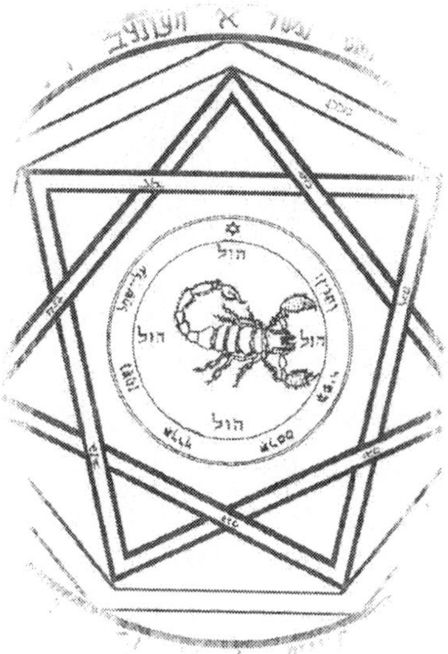

"Devil trap," Asar said, winking.

"Of course," Keith slowly whispered. He rose to his feet and began examining several symbols closer. "Storm's cabin?"

"Storm's cabin." Asar replied, smiling.

"Got it."

Keith reached out and ran his fingers over the lines and curves of light that had appeared. To his touch, the routes of illumination seemed to be part of the cabin's surfaces. He could find no visible channels or bulbs.

"What is it?" he asked, turning to address Asar.

"I told you," Asar began. "Protection... a devil trap... a..."

"No... no," Keith interrupted. "The light... what's it made of?"

"Magic," Asar said, laughing.

"Magic?"

Keith turned back to the wall and ran his open palm over the surface. "With a switch?"

"Magic with a switch, Mr. Keith."

"How does that work?"

SMASH!

Keith's pondering was interrupted by a calm-shattering impact at the door of the cabin. He threw himself back onto the couch and slid up against the side wall of the seat, eyes fixed on the door.

"Holy shit, Asar!"

SMASH! BANG!

"What do we do?" Keith cried over the onslaught at the threshold of their cabin.

Before Asar could reply, a horrid symphony of scratching and tapping set to work on their door. Keith could now hear the garbled echoes of moaning and crying sliding in and out of audible levels, like the stereophonic effects one might experience while wearing a pair of headphones. Keith's gaze fell upon the base of the cabin door as a slew of insects, spiders and scorpions crept and wedged their way under the tiny space. Keith backed up further into the recesses of the cabin, rising to his feet on the couch.

"Asar, what the fuck?!" he cried, turning to his companion, who appeared completely unphased by the display of crawling filth that was moving into their cabin.

Leaning forward in his seat, Asar peered down at the trove of creatures that had made their way into their quarters. Raising one eyebrow at Keith, he slowly lowered his body back against the cushiony pillows of his seat.

"Shouldn't we do something, man?!"

Asar shook his head and pointed up to the ceiling as the assault on the door began once more. The noise intensified to such an extent that Keith watched in horror as the door shimmied and creaked in its frame.

"ASAR!"

Keith's cries were silenced by a blinding exhibition of raining beams of light that fired throughout the room like lasers in a sci-fi flick. Veering from their brilliance with shut eyes, he steadied himself in the small corner he had backed into. After several seconds, Keith was able to register a cessation to the room's defensive maneuvers by the absence of the intense glow that had been permeating his eyelids. Prying them open against his better judgment, he found Asar smiling at him from across the table. The room was absent of the evil that had scampered over the threshold into their sanctuary. Keith also noted that the disturbance on the other side of the sleeper car's door had subsided as well.

"What the hell?"

Asar smiled. "Precisely... Lucky we have the U.S. military, no?"

"What?"

"The Star Wars... right?"

Keith's exasperation was not fading.

"What?"

"The defense system, Mr. Keith... Star Wars."

Asar lifted a hand and waved it about at the illuminated symbols and words.

Keith shook his head mockingly.

"We are quite safe, my friend." Asar's voice was comforting this time. "As I said, you have nothing to fear."

"Really? Well, that's nice to know..."

"Yes... quite comforting."

Keith settled down in his seat and claimed the bottle of water Asar had placed in front of him at some point. *While I'm panicking, Asar's handing out drinks*, Keith thought. He shook his head and took a gulp of cool water.

"What now, big guy?"

"Now," Asar said, as he shifted in his seat and extended his legs out across the couch, laying his head back on a pillow under the window. "Now, I suggest you get some rest. It would appear that the assistance we will be rendering to William may be more trying than I had first predicted."

"Really?" Keith was taken aback. "What gives you that impression?"

"Well, to start, the demonic entities that just tried to enter our cabin."

"That was rhetorical," Keith said, leaning back against the seat. "I was being sarcastic."

"So was I."

Asar sat up and cast him a serious eye, then dropped back into his prone position on the couch.

"Sorry," Keith replied, trying not to be disrespectful. "What does this tell you about where we're headed?"

"I am not sure." Asar had no insight to offer into their future situation. "But it does speak volumes towards one thing."

"Oh yeah?" Keith, truly exhausted, laid back on the couch as well. "What's that, big guy?"

"It tells us that Richard Pierpont's loyalties are... questionable... at best."

7

Alexander Storm stumbled from the ruins of the burnt-out theater onto the stone-paved street. Taking a deep breath, he leaned over with his hands on his thighs and tried to shake the evil essence that permeated his senses. Absently, his gaze wandered to the damp street stones at his feet.

"Belgium block," he snickered. "In Francia?"

The virtually full moon cast a tranquil luminescence across the night dew that coated the archaic roadway. Alex meditated on the brilliant imagery for a moment but was soon distracted by flashing high beams disrupting the moonlight. Storm lifted one arm and waived Doc off, for the moment.

Righting himself, Alex retrieved his cell and began to slowly tread in the opposite direction of his driver's waiting vehicle. Dialing, he held the phone to his ear and waited for the connecting ring. Several seconds ticked by and Alexander took the opportunity to compose himself fully.

"Alexander?" Kate's voice finally boomed through, and he smiled, gaining comfort from the familiar mixture of excitement and inquiry that was present in her tone.

"Yes," he said, his voice betraying him as it cracked, ever so slightly. He cleared his throat. "Yes, it's me."

"You okay?"

He could detect some concern filtering through the speaker to his ear.

"Are you okay?" Storm mimicked, fearing the call was a mistake so soon after his spectral encounter.

"Hah... uh, yeah... I'm okay." Kate stopped pacing at the base of the spiral staircase that led to the east tower of Dragon Loch Castle. "What's up, Alex?"

"Upon inquiry, the origins of which were derived from the notions and reports of a very old and dear acquaintance, a concerned and observant learned individual, you understand... I was away to a Parisian theater, as it were, at which time the melodramatic theatrics of a dime store student of prestidigitation morphed into something far more sinister and, I fear, legions of darkness are assembling... or perhaps are *being* assembled... and... madness is abounding, my dear."

"Alexander," Kate said to her mentor with maternally encapsulated words. "I have no idea what you're talking about."

"You don't?"

"Nope."

"I see."

"Well... I don't... I don't understand."

"Which part?"

Kate paused and covered the phone with palm of her hand as the conversation was becoming comical and she feared laughter would escape her lips.

"All of it, Alexander," she blurted out, covering the cell again.

"I see." Alexander shook his head to clear the last remnants of illusion from his mind.

"I don't." The tone of Kate's voice was becoming obvious.

"Don't what?" asked Alexander, a hint of unintentional annoyance echoing in his words.

"I *don't* see Alexander... I don't see... I don't understand... I can't even remember what you just told me, for God's sake."

"Okay, okay... no need to get uppity..."

"What!?"

"Withdrawn... my apologies." Alexander changed topics quickly, which Kate found more amusing than any of the other bits of dialogue they had just exchanged. "Are you at the east tower, Kate?"

"What?"

"You didn't understand that either?"

"Hey..." she shouted, faking offense.

"Off-limits," Alex instructed and moved on. "Serket?"

"Yes," Kate replied happy to the change of themes as well. "Philip received word she should arrive in the morning."

"Excellent." Alexander turned to look behind him and was surprised to see how far he had wandered from the car. His acute vision focused on the vehicle in the distance and then on its driver, who was now standing outside the car behind the open door. Storm could sense Doc's concern even from this distance, and he waved to him with his free hand in an effort to alleviate his apprehension. Doc returned the wave but remained stoic aside the vehicle.

"Well," Alex said, returning to Kate. "What of the others?"

"The others," she replied. "Keith and Asar left, and I haven't heard from them..."

"Yes, yes..." Alex hurried her on. "They are undertaking several tasks at my behest and will eventually meet up with William."

"Decker?!" Anger seethed from her words. "Keith failed to mention anything about Decker."

"Must have slipped his mind."

"Not likely."

"Perhaps, and I would surmise, as I am sure you have done already, that his failure to make mention of William was nothing more than his romantic efforts to assist you in avoiding worry."

"Well..." she stammered. Kate was taken aback by his bluntness, which she was learning, came in unpredictable waves, broken apart by smooth seas of mystery. "Since you put it that way..."

•

"He is relatively safe, my dear," Alexander reassured her. "Quite innocuous are the responsibilities I have ascribed to them."

"Relatively?"

"That is what I said."

"Relative to what? Say, battling legions of the dead in the shadow of the pyramids?"

"Correct."

"Jesus, Alex, you are really difficult tonight."

"Difficult?" Alex was offended. "I've barely said anything."

"Oh, no." She was getting pissed. "You said a lot... and it's amounted to nothing."

"Serket is in transit," Storm spoke over her continued complaints. "Asar and Keith are *safe* and shall return to us with William. What of Abigail?"

Kate huffed, surrendering to the fruitless exchange. "Abi is not due back for a week or so and..."

"That will not do," Alex interrupted. "When we hang up, call her straight away and advise her that I require her to cut her familial reunion short, and that she is to return to the Loch at once."

"What's going on?"

"I told you..." Alexander's voice grew shallow and he hesitated. "I'm not sure... but I need us all... together... okay?"

"Okay..." Her reply was solemn and compliant. She trusted Alexander and the gravity of whatever he was sensing. "I'll call her."

"I will text Philip and have him arrange immediate transport for her, so when you speak with Abi, tell her to be ready... please."

"Okay," she said, giggling. "Except I don't think Philip uses texts, Alex."

"Oh," His voice took on a proud tone. "He is quite proficient in social media and messaging... I taught him myself, Kate."

Kate laughed out loud. "Oh my God... really? Okay I'll help him after I speak to Abi."

Alexander ignored her insulant remarks. "What of our rebellious child?"

"She's not a child, Alexander."

"No, of course not," Storm said, smiling. "An allegory."

"Not really." Kate caught him off guard.

"It most certainly..." he stumbled. "No, I guess it is not an allegory."

"Man, you *are* off tonight. Should I be worried?"

"Never."

Kate smiled. "Of course not." She moved on. "I have messaged with Sam a bit... nothing extensive... she's hurting... still."

"We all are, my dear." Alex didn't skip a beat. "None more than I."

"You can't say that, Alex. I think that was part of the problem."

"How is that?"

"Her grief is different than yours, and to compare the two is offensive."

"I knew Lobo... I interacted with him, in one form or another, practically on a daily basis... for nearly twenty years, Kate."

"Different..."

"Yes, quite different from a thirty-minute puppy love story."

"Wrong," she shot back at him. "So wrong."

Alexander halted their conversation and began to walk back to Doc and his awaiting chariot.

Kate chose to break the silence. "What if it had been someone like Serket? Would Asar's loss have felt different in comparison to your grief?"

"That is quite a different set of facts and circumstances, Kate... you cannot compare ages of affection to something that developed under intense stress and lasted only several...."

"Stop!" she shouted into the cell. "You're wrong... don't even finish that statement. A person can love a lifetime in a single moment... perhaps loving more in that short time than an entire life spent together."

Alexander said nothing as he arrived at the black Lincoln. Doc, noting the cell phone at his ear, remained silent as he swiftly came around the passenger side and opened the back door. Storm nodded in appreciation and lowered himself on to the plush leather seats as Doc closed the door.

"Are you there?" Kate again broke the thick layer of silence that had settled in on their conversation.

"I was pondering your words," Alex replied with appreciative understanding. "Perhaps there is some level of truth in your analysis."

"Thank you," Kate sighed.

"I will speak to Samantha myself."

"You're sure about that?"

"Diplomacy be thy name..." Alex reached forward and tapped Doc on the shoulder as he situated himself in the driver's seat. "I will talk to Samantha."

"Okay, then." The excitement created by the possibility of a reunion between the two of them was transparent in her speech. "I'll work on Abi... are you returning home now?"

"Not quite yet." Alexander paused and signaled Doc to proceed out of the little village. "We have one stop to make first."

"Where?"

"I'll explain later." Alexander's shroud of mystery had returned. "Along with a more lucid account of the events of this evening."

"Right." Kate did not bother to protest. She knew their conversation was over and Storm's mind was already somewhere else.

"I will speak to you in short time, my dear," Alexander said, leaning forward in his seat again. "No east tower, Kate... Good night."

Kate did not have an opportunity to bid Alex farewell before she heard the rustle of cloth on the other end of the phone. He had forgotten to end their call before placing the cell back into his jacket and she shook her head at his absentminded nature. Removing her phone from her ear, Kate was about to hang up when the clearly discernable accent of Doc's voice audibly resonated from the speaker, and she held the phone back to her ear.

"Where to, boss?" Doc asked.

"Halifax... Nova Scotia," Storm instructed. "We need to pay a visit to a quaint little used bookstore on Windsor Street."

8

Samantha slammed the phone down on the charging dock and sprang from her chair. She was frustrated beyond belief with her current employer and was ready to scrap the job. She couldn't take any more of the Board's unrealistic demands with regards to schedules and deadlines. This routine was not what she had signed up for when N.A.G.A. Corp. had originally contracted her, and she wasn't really sure when the entire project has changed course.

The preliminary scope of her work consisted of basic code breaking, involving ciphers which required high-end mathematical equations to solve. They were functions well beyond the human mind, but mere child's play for a silicon brain. The computers did most of the work, and she had been able to turnaround the material ahead of N.A.G.A.'s expectations.

Several weeks ago, the primary mathematical solutions turned from number theory and abstract algebra to calculus-driven resolutions. Sam had re-evaluated the contract at that time and teetered on the idea of letting it go. The money was so damn good though that she just couldn't justify ending the relationship. The Board's extremely generous compensation had allowed her to upgrade her infrastructure with state-of-the-art equipment. She had even bought a new bike without selling her old one. Yup, she was now the proud owner of two motorcycles. *The things we aspire to*, she had thought at the time, amusing herself. And it truly was "herself." She was alone. Her daily life was purposely shrouded in solitude since returning home.

Rubbing her eyes, she gazed down at the printout of the most recent PDF N.A.G.A. had forwarded her. Standing above the sheet, Sam tried to find some pattern, a starting point, from the series of obscure angles and shapes that comprise the puzzle. This was no longer calculus. She had entered into the realms of some type of crazy-ass trig.

Turning abruptly, she crossed the studio apartment, and with the fervor of a pillaging Norseman, yanked open the hefty stainless-steel door of her new fridge (N.A.G.A. Corp. funded as well) and grabbed an ice-cold Corona from the top shelf. Slamming the door abruptly behind her, she took the Lord Vader bottle opener from the counter and expertly popped the top off. She took a big gulp and stretched her neck about before partaking in a second swig.

Closing her eyes, she laughed and shook her head in surrender. Returning to her worktable, she peered down over the upturned bottle at her mouth at the bizarre mathematical images.

Musing, she spoke to the empty apartment. "Looks more like an Alexander Storm puzzle than a computer hacker's..."

Her soliloquy was cut short by the ringing of her cell phone, the melody of which was becoming intolerable to her ears.

"Hello..." Her voice offered the caller both question and statement all at once. It was unintentional.

"Hello, Samantha."

Sam froze. Her silence, although no more than a second or two, seemed to linger eternally.

"Hello," she replied finally.

"How are you?" Alexander inquired.

"Peachy," she snapped. "What do you want?"

Storm chuckled uncomfortably. "Right to the point as always."

"Yup, what can I do for you, Storm?"

"I too will get to the point — directly," he started, but was interrupted.

"Appreciate it."

"Yes, well..." he began again. "I require the use of your services once more. Your assistance, as it were."

"Not a chance," Sam scoffed without hesitation.

"You haven't even heard what I have to say."

"Not interested, Storm." Her voice was cold, and Alexander considered allowing her to return to her solitude.

He thought better of it, however. "Enough, Samantha. We all miss him. But life must perpetuate... eternally... and now your presence is required once more."

Sam bit her tongue against the brash onslaught of responses that had instantly jumped up into her throat.

"I am not interested, Storm." She kept her cool. She wasn't going to give him the satisfaction. "Besides even if I wanted to, I have work... a job."

"I am well aware," he said, laughing.

"What the hell does that mean?"

"I am aware that you are actively working."

"Oh." She took another gulp of cold beer, dragging her forearm across her lips as she held the bottle out.

"I am sending a car for you Samantha. It will arrive within an hour or so. Be ready."

"I will not."

"You will. You are needed... I need you... I am imploring you to reconsider."

"As I said, I have work to do here."

Alex could hear her voice faltering. Perhaps it was her curiosity. Perhaps it was the loneliness of her self-imposed solitude. It mattered not - as long as she complied.

"Ah yes, N.A.G.A., correct?"

She could hear the spark in his voice. *What is he toying at,* she wondered.

"What?" Sam's anger finally broke through. Was he spying on her?

"Samantha, do us all a favor..." Alex's pace quickened. "You... me... Kate, who misses you dearly by the way..."

"What's that, Storm?"

"Remove the punctuation from your benefactor employer, run a search, pack your bags, and get in the car when it arrives."

"I told you..." Sam's voice grew louder.

"And be sure to bring your most recent project. It must be solved in due time. Goodbye, Samantha. I am afraid other matters now require my undivided attention."

The line went dead, and Samantha's face went red.

"What the fuck?!" she cried out, caught off-guard by his parting words. She dropped to her chair and allowed her fingers to orchestrate the keyboard.

"Remove the punctuation..." she repeated with hostility as she typed *NAGA* into the search bar.

She read the results in disbelief. *Indonesian for dragon. How could she have missed it?* "Storm! God damn it!"

Jamming her chair back, she rose to her feet with force and headed off in search of a duffle bag. Stopping suddenly, she pivoted on her biker boots and returned to the sheet of cryptic figures on her desk.

"Fucking Storm," she hissed as she swiped the sheet up and marched toward her closet with the swagger of a grounded teenager.

9

"We are here, my friend."

Asar had already sprung up and was at the door of the compartment. "I trust you slept well and are refreshed and ready to move, yes?"

Keith rose slowly from his inverted fetal position on the couch and extended his arms in the shape of a *V*. His jaw began its own version of stretching as he attempted to contain the yawn that persistently pressed through his smile.

"What?" he mumbled, blinking his eyes for clarity. It was then he saw Asar reaching for the slide lock on the cabin door and sprang to his feet.

"Wait," he cried, fumbling across the train car for Asar's arm.

"Get off me, boy!" Asar shook Keith's grip free and scowled at the panicking man's face. "Relax!"

"You can't." Keith threw his body against the door in comedic fashion as Asar took a step back and smiled.

"It's okay, my friend." Asar reached down and straightened the cuff of his jacket, then plucked several pieces of lint from the edge of his sleeve. In a gentlemanly fashion, rooted in the institutional education of his youth, Asar was giving pause to allow his companion to recover, and perhaps save face.

"How do you know?" Keith finally blurted out, his voice still wavering, but his composure returning.

Asar stepped towards the door abruptly and Keith jumped from his path. Before further objections could be raised, the door to the compartment was open and the hefty Egyptian was passing over the threshold. Keith watched with manic apprehension as Asar disappeared into the train car. He pressed his legs to move - to follow - but his feet were glued to the burgundy carpeting below. His mind's eye flashed with images of menacing Lovecraftian creatures just beyond his view. Keith conjured droves of insects and spiders swarming and festering in the shadows outside the realms of their compartment - sharp pincers, stingers dripping with venom, ready to pounce on their victim once he exited the sanctity of Alexander Storm's *magical* sleeper cabin.

"Are you coming?"

Asar's head popped back into the compartment, causing Keith's frozen feet to jump back, at last freed from their imaginary prison.

"Yeah... yup..." His motor functions working once more, he joined his companion in the hallway.

Asar laughed. "See? The entire car is empty. Nothing to fear here any longer."

Turning and heading towards the exit to the train, he was halted once more by Keith's grasp.

"How do you know... it's safe... I mean, how do you know?"

Asar yanked his arm free in a slow, unoffensive manner and resumed his steady march toward the exit. "I just know. Let's move it, my friend... we are on a schedule."

Asar opened the exit, and Keith sprinted to his side. There was no way he was getting left behind in the sleeper car from hell. Not happening. Moving past his companion, Keith descended the three steps to the wood platform of the station. His feet caused the weathered planks to creak with the addition of his weight, and he looked up at Asar.

"Where are we?" he asked, while apprising the unkempt state of his current surroundings and the utter lack of another human being amongst the rural ruins.

"Tunisia," Asar said, smiling. "Wonderful land."

Joining Keith on the platform, he took the lead and headed towards the road just visible on the other side of the small, dilapidated station house ahead of them.

"Where's Decker?" asked Keith, He was doing his best to keep up with the hulking man's strides. "I thought he would meet us here."

"Decker," Asar replied without slowing, "is otherwise occupied... and desperately needs us to go to him... not him to us."

Keith shook his head. Was it him, or was every word out this damn guy's mouth a fucking riddle? *Hey, how about one straight answer, one that doesn't require me to think, ponder or deduce, you pain in my butt,* the words flowed in his mind... but he decided to keep them to himself. Asar was huge, and although he was a tad bit older than Keith, just a tad, he was as tough as petrified driftwood... and just as salty, at times. He had bore witness to the hot-blooded Egyptian's lack of patience and tendency to flip his rage on and off like a light switch. No, he didn't think it was a good idea to piss Asar off.

"Can you give me some insight here? What are we headed into?"

"Not sure."

"Okay." Keith quickened his pace as Asar cut sharply to their right and bee-lined towards what he surmised passed for a cab in these parts. "What did you get from the chick in Morocco?"

"Chick?" Asar mimicked.

"The girl... in Marrakesh." It was a day ago - was he kidding?

"Oh, yes." Asar turned back to Keith, standing next to the open driver's window of the taxi now. "She gave us the object we need to bring to William."

Keith said nothing, closing his eyes for a moment in a heartfelt display of frustration. When he opened them, Asar was speaking, his voice low and deep, to the cab driver who motioned them into the back of a dusty old Toyota. As soon as Asar pulled their door shut, the vehicle took off, leaving the seemingly abandoned station in a burst of dirt and smoke.

Asar sat back in the seat and peered out the window at the landscape flying by.

His momentary peace was broken by the driver. "Where go?"

Keith looked at the driver's reflection in the sand-blasted glass of the rearview mirror. His beady black eyes and the oily bridge of his nose were the only view the thin mirror allowed him from his seat.

"Djerba," Asar offered dryly. "Les Maisons de la Mer resort."

Keith's body was hurled forward as the driver slammed on the brakes.

"Hey!" he cried out as he struggled to regain his balance and right himself on the seat. Asar's body did not react to the sudden stop.

"You not go there." The driver did his best to form his English sentences. "Not nobody go Les Maisons... nice place, very nice... there." The driver gestured to some unseen point in the distance.

"Shall we hail another cab?" Asar's eyes were transfixed on the rearview mirror now, studying the driver's expressions and mannerisms.

"No, no..." he said, taking his foot off the brake. "I go you there... no, no..."

The driver repeated himself several more times as he sped off again, headed towards some ungodly location specified by Keith's companion. Easing himself back against his seat, Keith marveled at the intermittent images of the businesses and homes they passed. Abandoned and crumbling structures stood side-by-side with well-maintained and elaborately designed ones.

"Sorry," the driver called out as he took a sharp bend in the road and tossed Keith against the side window. Once again, Asar's body sat stoically.

The cab traveled for over thirty minutes in relative silence through a much less developed stretch of highway, emerging eventually into a concrete sea of majestic hotels and resorts.

Asar remained silent as the driver brought the car to a sudden stop at the side of the road and the front passenger door sprang open with a metallic creak. Keith's brow wrinkled as he watched a shadowy hooded figure drop into the seat in front of him. Turning to Asar, Keith opened his mouth to speak, but was silenced by the raised palm Asar flashed him at seat level.

"Is ok, right?" The driver did not turn nor look up at the mirror. "He go same way, yes?"

Asar stared straight ahead out the front windshield and slowly shimmied his body into the middle of the rear bench seat of the car. Like a bullet, they sped off again, traveling at a high rate of speed over the dusty pavement. Keith turned to Asar again, panic in his eyes at the strange reaction of his companion.

Asar tried to get the attention of the newly arrived passenger, who remained non-responsive and motionless. "Where are you headed, my friend?"

The dark flowing folds of the passenger's garb hid his features from their view.

"Are we in trouble?" Keith asked as quietly as possible. Asar did not reply or look at him.

"I say again, man," Asar said, leaning forward now. "Where is it you are heading?"

"What, I wonder," came forth the words like a whisper on the wind, "does it have in its pocket?"

Keith, shocked by the sound of the dark passenger's voice, pressed himself further back into his seat. His panicked mind, short-circuiting as it was from his ignorance of what was going on, couldn't help but think of Gollum echoing Bilbo's riddle in the dark, gloomy depths of the Misty Mountains.

What does it have in its filthy... little...

Keith's thoughts came to a grinding halt, as did the car, and the whispering figure from the front seat twisted around towards the back seat. His ebony-cloaked body rose unnaturally and lurched forward in an attempt to leap into the rear of the cab. Keith noticed Asar's movements in the outer edges of his peripheral vision and reflexively turned his attentions to his companion. Asar's hands lay crossed across his chest, hands secreted under the folds of his coat. Keith's eyes shot back towards the front and tracked the trajectory of the lurching figure, who sailed through the air like a bellowing mass of shadows. The creature's flowing hood continued to obscure what lay beneath. Keith strained the limits of his vision until he was able to discern the blurred mappings of a lower jaw and cheek which appeared melted and burnt.

Keith realized that crippling panic was consuming his limbs but was granted a reprieve by the sight of Asar's hands withdrawing from his coat. Uncrossing his arms as they extended forward, Asar leapt up to meet the attack with a silver blade in his right hand and a pistol in his left. With mastered choreography, in one fluid motion Asar plunged the blade into the recesses of the creature's hood and fired a single shot into the side of the driver's head. Keith froze in horror as a mist of blood painted the front windshield as the driver's head burst like a melon under a mallet. The cabbie cadaver slumped sideways, and his mangled head landed in the dark figure's lap.

"AHHH!" Asar screamed out, releasing his grip on the handle of the blade that had become wedged into the skull of whatever manner of creature sat in the passenger seat. The handle glowed bright red, and Keith stared in awe at the seared impression of the blade's grip branded into Asar's palm.

"Get out, you fool!" he yelled at Keith, who instinctively pulled the handle on the door and fell out. Hitting the road hard, he hastily righted himself and scurried backwards like a crab on the run to the surf. Asar jumped across the seat and out the open door of the cab as the figure in the passenger seat began to radiate beams of intense light, which transformed into flames that dissolved the dusty cloak and hood that donned its body. The two watched as the fire's intensity continued to grow until the entire vehicle was ablaze.

Asar rose to his feet and extended an outstretched hand to Keith. Grasping him by the shoulder, he helped his frightened companion to his feet and the two moved a safe distance from the burning car. Asar symbolically dusted the dirt and debris from Keith's chest and tapped him with an open palm.

"We walk from here," Asar instructed, and set out down the deteriorating road.

"Ya think?" Keith replied, falling in behind the Egyptian warrior.

10

Alexander pivoted back and forth, peering up and down the dimly lit pathways of Windsor Street. He found himself taken by the stillness of the night, his gaze lingering for a time into the darkness of the deserted road.

"Everything all right, boss?" Doc had opened the door to their car and was standing at its side.

"Remain in the vehicle," Storm replied without turning to face him. "Honk," he said, hesitating as he contemplated the form of his next words, "if anything seems out of the ordinary."

"Out of the ordinary, like...?"

"Anything that does not seem ordinary." Alex's voice, dry as it was, echoed with the sentiments of condescending sarcasm, and Doc stretched his eyes wide in surprise at his tone.

Alexander listened to his own words as they replayed in his mind and turned to his driver. Offering Doc a wink and the slightest hint of a smirk, he spun and headed towards the front entrance of the quaint Halifax bookshop.

The storefront consisted of a glass-paneled wood door, framed by large paned windows on either side. Alex headed to the left side first and leaned into the glass. Shielding the dim glare of the closest streetlamp with the palm of his hand, he strained his eyes to see the interior. Years of dust and weathering, coupled with the complete absence of illumination from within, made his efforts fruitless.

From behind him, the snap of the car door as Doc returned to the driver's seat broke Alex's trance, and he stepped away from the window and headed to the front door of the bookstore. Several strands of yellow tape blocked the threshold, and Alex tilted his head to read the black writing that repeated itself across the plastic ribbon.

RCMP – H DIVISION – DO NOT CROSS.

Storm averted his eyes momentarily and allowed a slight burst of air to escape his lips before swiping the crime scene tape from the entranceway. Reaching out, he grasped the decorative brass handle and attempted to rotate it in either direction. The door was securely locked. Sliding his hand into the inner pockets of his long jacket, he retrieved a small green leather pouch and unsnapped the flap. Crouching down to eye level with the handle, Alex inserted the dual metal arms of the lock pick into the keyhole of the handle. Within seconds the faint click of submissive cylinders could be heard in the still night, and Alex stood up. Pushing the door open, Storm's body reacted to the haunting tune of the brass doorbell hanging above the frame. Quickly regaining his composure, he stepped into the musty air of the shop and closed the door behind him, causing the bell to echo through the dark silence once more.

Making good use of the bright LED light on his phone, Alexander began to navigate his way through the rows of rare volumes. The books appeared untouched since De Molay's untimely departure from this world, and Alex mused at the scatterbrained cataloging techniques of his eccentric old friend. Stopping at the center of the store, Alex moved around to the back of the counter as the chalk outline of his comrade's body came into view. Storm crouched and directed his light over the forensic markings as a glimmer of metal caught his eye. Illuminating the space above the head of the outlined figure, he revealed the source of the reflection. A faint smile crept across his face as he wrapped his fingers around the handle of the fallen knight's blade.

"A warrior to the end, my old friend," he uttered to the darkness as he rose upright. "A warrior to the end."

Alexander's momentary feelings of solace were quickly replaced with apprehension as he spotted the dislodged floorboard at his feet. Using the tip of the sword, Alex flipped the loose panel to the side and shone his light into the barren space beneath.

"Naamah," the words left his throat as a whisper, and he shook his head. "Such a waste, my friend."

Returning to his search, Alex turned his attention to the rear of the shop. Walking along the rows of shelves that lined the back wall, he suddenly stopped at several piles of books that were strewn across the floor at his feet. Tracing the scattered trail to its point of origin, his light stopped on a large wooden chest. Storm surmised that someone had brushed the books aside to gain access to the steamer chest and its contents. He moved cautiously around to the front of the trunk and spotted the unlatched steel lock on the floor. Inhaling deeply, Storm once again made use of the sword's tip and flipped the chest's lid open. Illuminating the interior, he dropped to one knee and peered inside. The sole content of the chest was a small wooden box.

Alex leaned the sword against the chest and retrieved the diminutive box. He studied its design and swiftly deduced it was quite ancient. Lifting off the lid, Alex shifted his grip on the items in his hand in order to position the focus of his light. The velvet-lined interior was empty save for a small slit in the fabric. The ring the box once housed was now gone.

BEEEEEP

Alexander replaced the cover on the ring box and slid it into his pocket. Taking hold of De Molay's sword, he doused the phone's light and swiftly made his way through the murky darkness of the bookstore. Peering out the window at the front entrance, Alexander watched as Doc threw open his door and began to rise to the side of the car. As he did, he leaned on the vehicle's horn once more.

BEEEEEP

Storm pulled open the door, causing the bell to chime surreally as he stepped into the balmy night air.

"What is it?" he demanded in a loud whisper, and Doc turned to him. Alexander immediately noted the insipid nature of his driver's complexion, which was evident to him even in the color-strained confines of the night.

"Would you classify *that* as *out of the ordinary*?"

Alexander Storm followed the path of the driver's pointing finger up Windsor Street to his right, and stood speechless for but a moment before darting towards the vehicle.

"Yes!" he shouted as he yanked open the back door of the car and dove in. "I believe you have mastered the terminology, my dear fellow!"

11

"It is wonderful to see you again Kate." Serket smiled across the table as she lifted the glass of red wine to her lips. "Ahhh... I needed that."

Kate laughed at Serket's exaggerated expression and reached across and touched the warrior's hand. "I missed you, Serket. I'm so glad you came."

She nodded. "Alex said it was urgent, and it is not often that he claims a situation is *urgent*, so here I am."

Kate sat back in her seat. She was obviously missing something.

"Wait," she started. "Storm called you here?"

Serket's eyes narrowed. "Yes..." She spoke the word slowly and it resonated with inquisition.

"Hmmm..." Kate's face wore a puzzled expression as she slowly pushed her chair back and rose to her feet. Serket watched her begin to pace the long dining room table, seemingly lost in her thoughts.

"Sit," Serket requested, following another sip of wine. "You are making me nervous, Kate... talk to me."

Kate did not comply immediately. She paused and stared at the deep brown eyes of her companion. She marveled at the perfection created by the Egyptian's mingling of beauty and might. She radiated a feminine force that rivaled Storm's omnipresence, and she achieved it with fierce grace.

"Sorry," she finally replied, and returned to her seat. "Philip, and Alexander for that matter, indicated, or at the very least alluded to the fact that you had decided to *visit* Dragon Loch." She paused to pour herself a small glass of the deep burgundy wine. "Neither of them mentioned you had been summoned here."

"Summoned?" Serket amplified her voice. "No one has summoned me anywhere."

"That's not what I meant," Kate quickly corrected. "You were asked to come to Dragon Loch. You didn't choose to come of your own accord."

Serket peered at her with one raised eyebrow. Kate's words were not landing in unison with her thoughts, and she was becoming frustrated.

"I'm not insinuating that Alex beckoned and you came..."

"That is exactly what occurred," Serket interrupted, "but it was my choice to come."

Kate smiled, nodding her head, "Of course. I just meant I didn't know he had called you. I was under the impression that you had decided to pay us a visit."

"I understand," Serket said with a smirk. "What does it matter, anyway?"

"Well," Kate began, "I thought your visit was social, but now it sounds like there's something going on which requires attention... attention that is concerning not only the great Alexander Storm, but also you. Something that tends to remind me of the events that transpired a short time ago, and well... honestly..."

Serket smiled and a comforting laugh escaped her lips, signaling to Kate that perhaps she was guilty of over-analyzing the situation. "Moloch and Naamah are gone, Kate... pretty sure that was a one-way ticket that Alex punched."

"So... what's going on, then?"

"Cheese," Philip announced as he entered the great dining hall from the side door to the kitchen. "Some quite pungent, unfortunately," he said with a laugh as he shuffled towards the table.

The women looked at each other and laughed with their eyes. Philip placed a large tray of cheese, olives, and jellies between them. "I shall fetch some biscuits, my ladies, and you shall partake in some very splendid accompaniments to that vino."

Serket grinned up at him. "Wonderful... just what the doctor ordered."

"Yes, well..." Philip tried his best to stifle his pleasure at her pleasure. "I shall be right back."

"Honey," she called out just before he exited the room.

"Pardon me?" He froze in his tracks and turned back to the table.

Serket spun in her chair to face him. "Honey... would you be a dear and bring some honey as well?"

Philip laughed nervously and nodded. "Of course."

Serket lifted her crystal wine glass from the table and giggled at Kate as the cup touched her lips.

Kate smiled. "You're so bad."

"Ah, he loves it." Serket placed the glass down in front of her and cut a small sliver of cheese from one of the wedges on the tray. "So... what is with all the concern here, Kate?"

Kate shifted uneasily. "There's got to be some kind of major issue, right?"

"No."

"No?" Kate looked puzzled.

"Nope." Serket took a bite of the cheese she was holding. By her expression, it appeared to please her pallet. "Perhaps a gathering."

"A gathering?"

"Yes, my dear... a get together, you know?"

Kate looked confused.

"A party."

"Oh." Kate squinted and pondered the revelation, smiling. "You think so?"

Serket took another sip of wine before responding. "No, I don't think that is why I am here... but it sounded nice."

Kate shook her head.

Serket leaned forward. "Look, there is no reason for us to sit here and worry about what is going on. Neither of us knows. Why not catch up and enjoy the company until Mr. Storm returns and illuminates us? What do you say... shall we?"

Kate thought for a moment and smiled. "I'll do my best."

"That'a girl."

"I'm sure it has something to do with that damn east tower," Kate mumbled as she reached for her glass.

Serket paused mid chew. "What?"

"Oh nothing." Kate took a sip. "I just noticed Alexander has been visiting the east tower quite often and keeps it locked and off-limits."

"It *is* off-limits, Kate." The serious nature of her tone mimicking Storm's own voice whenever he would reiterate the warning.

"You know..." she said, sitting up in her tall-backed chair. "You know what's going on up in the tower, don't you?"

"Up? No." Serket returned to her drink.

"Huh?" Kate replied. "What do you mean, up?"

"It is for Alexander to explain."

Serket shook her head and turned, seemingly startled, toward the sound of Philip re-entering the room.

"Honey," he called out as he moved towards the women.

Serket smiled in response. "Dear."

Philip's cheeks grew ruddy with involuntary heat, and he set down a covered basket containing crackers and biscuits in-between them. Bowing slightly in Serket's direction, he presented the Egyptian beauty with a small canister of golden amber.

Philip smiled and handed her a honey dipper. "For your assistance."

"Thank you so much, Philip. This is perfect."

Philip's grin grew ear-to-ear, pleased with his own efforts, and he turned to take his leave.

"Thank you," Kate called out as he made his way toward the kitchen.

"Of course, Miss Kate," he shouted without turning. "Of course."

Kate smiled at Serket, eyes wide in overstated emotion. "Well, looks like I just got knocked from his number one slot."

Serket laughed. "Fear not... I shall eventually depart."

The two laughed a bit, ate a bit, and drank a bit more.

"So, the tower..." Kate eventually returned to her obsessive inquiry.

"I can certainly see why Alexander likes you."

"Yeah, O.C.D... The east tower?"

"All I can tell you," Serket began.

"Yes?" Kate, her mind warm with wine, could barely contain herself. "Sorry," she said, grimacing at her own interruption.

Serket nodded empathetically and continued. "All I can tell you is that the space located beneath the east tower is deep, and it existed long before Dragon Loch stood upon these shores."

"OMG," Kate exclaimed. "How deep?"

"Fathoms."

"Okay..." Kate excitedly stood and moved around the table to the empty chair on Serket's left. "What's down there, Serket? What lies 'fathoms' below Dragon Loch?"

As Kate waited with bated breath, Serket replied "I... have no idea."

"Oh, come on!" Kate cried out, throwing herself back into the chair. "You're lying."

"Never," Serket replied with a comical abundance of insult at her companion's accusation.

"Come on," Kate begged once more. "What's down there?"

"I really don't know."

"Okay." She was going to dissect Serket's words with a tipsy version of twenty questions. "Have you ever been in the tower?"

Serket pondered the question. "Up, not down."

"Up?" Kate repeated as if getting somewhere on her quest for forbidden knowledge. "And when you walked through the locked door, that is, when you had occasion to enter the east tower and you walked through the door, were there steps leading both up and down?"

"Nope."

"Huh..." Kate was confused by Serket's response. "How's that?"

"There were only steps up the tower - spiral stone steps winding against the outer wall of the tower."

"I see..." Kate considered her next question a moment as Serket returned to her wine. "Do you know how to descend the tower?"

Serket smiled slyly. "Sure... you climb the steps to the top, and then you follow them back down... descending the tower."

"Ahhh," Kate replied with dismay, caught by the formation of her question. "Do you know how to descend the tower from the entry point behind the locked door?"

Serket smirked. "Yes."

Kate interpreted her smile as an indication that she was once again walking into an answer that would be unhelpful due to the non-specific nature of her question. "Hold on, hold on..."

"I'm not going anywhere."

"This is some Gollum and Bilbo-level give-and-take here." Kate laughed, thoroughly enjoying herself despite her growing frustrations.

Serket nodded. "Yes... but tell me..."

"Yes?"

"Which of us is supposed to be Gollum?"

Kate chuckled and returned to her line of inquiry. "So you enter the tower through the locked door..."

"Okay."

"You can't descend the 'fathoms' from that location?"

"Correct."

"So, you can only climb up... ascend... from the locked entryway?"

"Right again," Serket said, smiling.

"Okay." Kate rubbed her hands together like a cartoon version of an evil genius. "Now we're getting somewhere."

"We are." Serket made an unimpressed grimace at Kate.

"Yes," Kate quickly confirmed. "We're getting somewhere."

"Not down," Serket teased.

"So, you ascend the stone staircase to... what?" Kate continued, doing her best to ignore Serket's ribbing.

"A room."

"A room!" Kate repeated with fervor. "A room."

"Yes," Serket confirmed. "There is a large circular room towards the top of the tower."

Kate's eyes grew wide with excitement. "What type of room? What is it?" she practically shouted.

"It's the *Red Room*," a voice called out from behind Kate and Serket, and they spun in their chairs to find Sam strolling towards them, a large olive-green duffle slung over her shoulder. "Alexander Storm's Red Room," she said, grinning.

"Sam!" Kate sprang from her chair and darted across the dining hall.

"Not in *that* part of the castle, he doesn't." Serket winked at Sam and rose from her chair as well.

"Touché." Samantha winked back, struggling to maintain her balance as Kate squeezed her with a bear-like embrace.

"Miss Samantha Sinclair." Philip trotted into the room behind Sam, winded by his pursuit after the castle's newest arrival.

Sam smiled. "Yeah, I think they got it, Jeeves."

"Philip," he hissed. "And I am *not* a butler, you foolish little woman."

The three women turned in unison and stared at Philip, who, in a moment of emotional cowardice, threw his hands in the air, essentially waving the trio off.

"I'll *fetch* another glass." Spirit broken, Philip turned towards the kitchen entrance.

Sam laughed and walked to Serket. "Good to see you." She smirked and tossed her bag down behind the chair at the head of the table.

"You as well," Serket replied with a smile.

"So..." Sam claimed Kate's chair as the others took a seat on either side of her. "What's with this tower... and why the hell am I here?"

12

Jericho pulled the handle on the door of the old jeep and pushed it out. He had barely risen from the passenger seat when Aptera's hand yanked at his shoulder, dragging him back into the passenger seat with force.

"Hey..." the Egyptian guide whispered vehemently as he reached up and slid the switch that doused the cabin light the open door had activated. "Easy, man," he instructed as he relinquished his grasp of Jericho's flannel shirt.

"Sorry," Frank said as he exited the Jeep, nodding in acknowledgment of his carelessness.

The two had ventured deep into the southern realm of the Egyptian state. They had traveled under the cloak of darkness to the Nile-engulfed island of Philae, and to be discovered now would surely result in detainment. Storm had given Jericho a brief history lesson on the location before sending him on his quest, explaining how the island had been consumed by the Nile, monuments and all, when the Aswan High Dam had been built in the 1960s. UNESCO had stepped in, and over many decades, moved most of the Temples and monuments to the nearby Island of Agilkia. The massive engineering feat was begun in the 1970s and included the relocation of the Temple of Isis. The Temple's remaining submerged remnants were the focus of Jericho's inquiry, as they possibly concealed the subject of Storm's directive.

"We must be gone by daybreak, Mr. Jericho." his guide was nervous, and the incessant reminders were beginning to make Frank jumpy.

"Not a problem, my friend," he replied, slinging the silver scuba tank over his shoulder. The weight of the apparatus caught him off-guard, causing his boots to sink further into the desert sand. Catching his balance, he reached into the open back of the Jeep and grabbed his diving mask. Sliding it over his head, he reassuringly winked at Aptera and perched the mask in the tightly cropped hair above his forehead.

"You point me in the right direction, and I'll do my thing." Jericho returned to the rear of the Jeep one last time and clutched a pair of black rubber flippers with his free hand. "We'll be back to the village before morning," he added, pivoting towards the dark water. "I promise."

"As you say."

The reluctant guide stepped past him and clicked on a flashlight, focusing the beam on the ground before them. The light's radiance pitched off the sun-bleached sand and illuminated the churning waters where the shores of the Nile kissed the waters of Lake Nassar.

Jericho shrugged and set out behind the guide. He had to remind himself of where they were and why his companion was so nervous. They trekked to the crossroads of many a precarious marauder. The concern was multi-faceted. There were the "good guys," the police and military, as well as the life-and-death dangers of roaming bands of nomads and sand tribes - not to mention revolutionaries and outright terrorists, all of whom thrived in the secluded, unpopulated regions of the Sahara.

"We'll be fine," Jericho quietly called out to his guide. The words were just as much for his own reassurance as his companion's.

Aptera stopped a few inches from the pulsing water and turned to Frank. Motioning him with the light's beam, he made a circular ring over an area of the dark water. The waves here were angrier than Jericho had expected, a product of the merging bodies of water, he assumed, and the descent would not be quite as simple as he had planned.

"Shit!" Jericho dropped the flippers into the sand and turned to look back at the Jeep, which was forty or so yards away.

"What?" Aptera anxiously shined the light on Frank's face. "What is it?"

"I forgot the light, man," he said, shaking his head. This guy was jamming up his mojo. "In the back of the Jeep."

Aptera's arm shot out across Jericho's chest as he attempted to make his way back, "I get," he commanded. "You get ready."

Nodding in agreement, Frank dropped the tank and gear from his shoulder, allowing it to rest in the sand of the shoreline. Repositioning himself, he hoisted it up again and put his arms through in the same fashion one dons a jacket from behind. Reaching around in the darkness he found the hanging straps and secured the scuba tank to his body. Using the toe of his boot, he wedged it against the heel of the other, and kicked one boot off. His bare foot came to rest in the soft sand, which remained warm to the touch. He repeated the process with his naked toes and removed the remaining boot, kicking it from his foot to the side of the shore. Looking over his shoulder, he was pleased to find Aptera heading back with the underwater light apparatus in hand.

Jericho pulled off his sweatpants, exposing the wet suit pants below them, as well as the large hunting knife strapped to his leg. Throwing his pants on top of the boots, he bent down and secured the flippers on his feet and waddled to the water's edge like a clumsy duck.

"You must hurry," his guide started again.

"Look," Jericho said, swiping the light from Aptera's hand. "Relax, okay? You're making me jittery."

The guide waved him off and pointed the light into the murky waves once again. "There," he whispered. "Look round there."

"I got it." Jericho reached around and grabbed the tank's regulator and put the mouthpiece between his teeth. Breathing in and out several times, he confirmed the equipment's smooth flow of oxygen.

"I got it," he mumbled through the mouthpiece's impediments, and instinctively offered his companion a thumbs up before entering the desolate waters.

Aptera's dark pupils followed the green glow of Jericho's light as it descended into the Nile's depths. "Allah protect the arrogant fool."

13

"Stop!" Alexander ordered, tapping the back of Doc's seat calmly.

"What?"

"Apply pressure to the brake pedal." Storm's even tone caused Doc to glance at his passenger in the rearview mirror to insure he was in fact serious about his instructions. He was.

Doc slammed the brake down, causing the car to come to a screeching halt. The faint odor of rubber quickly filled the interior. Alex clenched his muscles in a futile attempt to maintain his body's position on his seat. His efforts resulted in him leaning forward rather than an all-out slam into Doc's seat.

"You okay?" Doc threw the transmission into park and rotated in his seat to get a better view of Alexander.

"Splendid." Alex was already pulling on the door handle, causing Doc to panic, blurting out a series of unintelligible questions and adjectives, as he rapidly tried to get out his door before Storm.

"Woohoo...?" Doc rose up next to the car. "What the hell, Storm?"

Alexander was already several steps away from the vehicle when he stopped to shoot his driver a stern look. "Excuse me?"

"Sorry, sorry..." Doc did his best to recover, waving his arms in a manner aimed at defusing the harshness of his words. "Sorry, boss..." he stammered, searching for the proper phraseology. "It's just..." He continued to stumble, but finally decided on reality rather than sugar-coated apologies. "THAT!" Doc cried, pointing up the road.

Alexander nodded at him dismissively and turned to face the apparition that was approaching. Steady and fierce, the private cyclone of smoke and fire spun like a whirling dervish on a collision course with their vehicle. The miniature tornado stood approximately twelve feet high and was wide enough to fill the small Nova Scotian Road from side-to-side. Kinetic sparks emanated at its base where the snout of its funnel danced upon the pavement. Echoing cries and hollow screams broke free from the spinning vacuum and sailed across the air to their ears, intensifying the dramatic, almost surreal, nature of the weather spectacle.

Alexander took a step back, unconsciously, and glanced over his shoulder at his driver. The fear on his face was real. The evil anomaly, small as it was in comparison to the grand tornadoes depicted in storm chaser videos, was devouring everything in its path.

"I think we should go, sir..." Doc moved to Alexander's side. "Now!"

Alex shook one finger at his driver, commanding both silence and patience.

"Storm!" Doc cried out with growing force. "Storm, we really should..."

"Wait!"

The pair watched on in terror as the tornado approached the patch of road in front of the bookstore, then suddenly ceased its forward march. Alexander nodded his head, a snicker escaping his lips.

"What?" Doc demanded. "What's going on?"

Maintaining his silence, Alex took several steps forward towards the stalled beast of wind and fire, which continued to rotate in place.

"It's not here for us..." he said, the words barely audible. "It's not here for us," Storm repeated with self-assured conviction.

"What? How do you know? We can't stay... we have to..."

"Look." Alexander nodded at the cyclonic display. The volume of the awful cacophony of lamenting souls intensified as the pair watched the beast of wind expand in both height and girth.

"My God!" Doc cried, grasping at Alexander's arm. "Please," he implored, "let's get out of here!"

The spinning fury finally broke free of its stagnating chains and cut a sharp path towards the front of the bookstore.

Alexander gasped. "It means to destroy the Templar Knight's sanctuary. Why?"

The two men watched in awe as the storm surged in magnitude until it towered above the small shop, galloping forward, until the building was completely engulfed by the destructive vehemence. The diabolical winds inserted their invisible fingers into every crevice of the structure and began to tear it limb from limb. First to go was the old slate roof. Slivers of stone scattered across the landscape like airborne missiles, causing Alex and Doc to seek cover behind the car to avoid their wrath.

Once the demonic wind had decapitated the structure, it took to the contents of the storefront, sucking the volumes of books and papers up into the night air, shredding and burning as it funneled them through. Like confetti at a ticker-tape parade, the scraps of shop contents floated down to earth around the watching pair.

Finally, with an awesome sound, the tempest imploded the walls of brick and wood inward upon themselves, leveling the old bookshop once and for all. Alexander stood upright from his crouched position, dismayed at the complete loss of such a significant site. The marauding winds made one last movement, turning and jolting at their location, before disintegrating in a burst of smoke and lightning mere inches from them.

Doc joined Alexander at the front of the car, dazed by the supernatural display he had just witnessed.

"My God," he echoed once more. "Have you ever encountered anything like that before?"

"Actually," Alexander began, as he brushed and dusted the flecks of scattered debris from his long coat, "I have... and quite recently, at that."

"For real?"

"Yes... for real," he assured, beginning to move towards the rear door of the car. "But I am fairly confident that this melodramatic display of phantasmic prowess has no relation to those events which recently transpired."

"Oh, yeah?" Doc, recognizing that it was time to go, double-stepped to the driver's side door. "How's that, Mr. Storm?"

Alexander pulled the rear door open and paused, staring at Doc from across the roof of the vehicle. "Because the unholy sorceress who last conjured such a display for her amusement... no longer walks amongst us."

14

"Are you sure you know where you're going, big guy?" Keith wiped the salt-rich sweat from his forehead as he picked up his pace.

Asar ignored his companion's doubtful concerns. He was preoccupied with the ruined corners and deserted alley spaces that comprised the abandoned remains of the Tunisian resort district. The skeletal remnants of once lavish hotels littered the landscape. The street they traveled on was in a severe state of disrepair. Potholes, road edge weathering, and vegetation overgrowth had devoured the once bustling thoroughfares of this holiday town. Sun shifts and clouds cast ominous shadows from every corner, and the ocean wind whispered across vacant doorways speaking in the language of despair and desolation.

"Hey!" Keith called out again.

Asar stopped short and spun around. "What, Keith?" His voice was filled with exasperation. "What is it?"

Keith, all at once shocked by his companion's recognition of his presence, stood blank-faced for several seconds before recovering. He took several fast-paced steps and joined Asar in the dwindling patch of shade the large man had purposely paused in.

"Asar," he said, his voice calmer now, "what the hell *was* that, man?"

"What?" Asar scrunched his eyebrows together in an almost comical attempt at ignorance.

"Really? Come on... the taxi?"

"Oh yes... demons, I would surmise... but you are no longer a neophyte with regards to these matters, are you?"

"Well..." Keith felt a wave of foolishness rush over him. "Yes, I suppose..."

"Then can we get on with it," the Egyptian said, cutting him short. "William is in need of our assistance, and by my calculations, we are behind schedule."

"I wasn't trying to delay reaching Decker." Keith's words echoed defensively. "I just want to know what's going on."

"I have no idea what's going on, Keith." Asar exited the patch of shadow. "Our mission is singular at this juncture."

Keith nodded and trotted to his side. "Sorry, what are we looking for? Is he in one of these abandoned resorts?"

"Yes."

"Which one?"

"I don't know."

Keith opened his mouth in what was surely to be another round of protest, but Asar headed him off at the pass.

"His jeep," Asar blurted out.

"His what?"

"William's jeep... we are looking for his jeep. It will be positioned outside of his location."

"Okay!" Keith shouted, thrilled to be privy to the *plan*, a sliver of intel to satiate his overwhelming feelings of ignorance. "Now see, *that* is information I can work with."

"Fine." Asar waved him off. "Help me find the jeep."

"You got it... I'll take the right side of the road, you take the left. We can split down side streets and join together as they pass. We'll cover more ground that way."

"No," Asar replied sternly. "We do not separate... understand?"

"Yeah, yeah... Easy. I'm just trying to help."

"Excellent." Asar peered down another passing side street. "Help in silence."

Keith snarled at his companion's intensifying foul mood. He just wanted to be part of the process.

"Are you lost?"

The child's voice froze the blood in Asar's veins, and he turned quickly towards its source. Keith too had been shaken by the unexpected break in their solitude, spinning so fast he almost threw himself off-balance, stumbling and contorting every muscle in his lower body to maintain his upright position.

The child's laughter filled the desolate remains of the street, echoing in all directions as it bounced off the empty buildings that encapsulated them. There was nothing foreboding to the small girl's amusement at Keith's spastic movements, and, once he had regained control of his muscles, he smiled at their guest.

"Hello." Keith could not help but offer the grinning little girl a peaceful, non-threatening greeting.

"Hi," she quickly replied. A thick amalgam of accent enriched her voice.

Asar walked past his companion and approached the child forcefully. To his surprise she did not shy away, but rather, her smile widened, and she extended a deeply tanned, albeit dirty, little hand up to Asar.

The towering Egyptian looked down at the child's hand, puzzled at first, and then took it softly in his own.

"Azrael," she said, and she shook his hand heartily. "Pleased to meet you."

Asar's body jerked with internal musing, and he returned her smile. "I am Asar." His voice had been transformed into something just shy of baby talk. "And this goofy fellow is Keith."

Keith smiled. "Hey... what's up?"

"Hello, Keith." She greeted each in turn. "Hello, Asar."

Finally letting go of his warm, meaty hand, Azrael took a minor step in reverse, gazing back and forth at the strangers. Her long dark hair twirled and bounced about her face, caught in the gusts of ocean breezes that intermittently came across the apocalyptic landscape. The silky wisps worked as camouflage on the cheeks of her face, masking the dust and grime that had collected there. Her dress, once white and adorned with embroidery of colorful flower petals, was now grey and dingy. The lower hem was frayed to shreds and the half sleeves ripped and stained. Her soil crusted toes were shoeless, unprotected from the scorching punishment of the sun-scorched pavement.

Asar noted her complexion, which did not resonate with the likes of any of the local peoples, and he surmised her to be of South American or perhaps even Italian descent. Most stunning, amidst the filth and wear, was her saucer-like deep brown eyes, which peered up at Asar with a mixture of joy and reservation.

"Well, it is very nice to meet you, Azrael." Asar spoke jovially in hopes of dispelling whatever worries were passing through the child's mind.

"So," she asked again playfully, "are you guys lost, or what?"

"Are you?" Keith interjected, stepping forward.

"Nope," Azrael said, laughing. "I live here."

"Where?" Asar proceeded cautiously, a sliver of doubt still resonating in his stubborn mind, no doubt a product of decades of Storm-based encounters. Alexander was a magnet for madness - so much so that the unexpected became the expected.

"Anywhere I want, silly." Laughing, she lifted her hands to the sky. "There's nobody else here."

"How did you get here, then?" Keith asked, his own cautionary senses still clinging to his vocal cords.

Azrael's face took on a confused look, and she averted her eyes to the ground. "I don't remember..." The breath of her words labored as they merged with her own puzzled thoughts. "I've just always been here."

Asar, still unsure of exactly what was transpiring, decided to change the topic.

"We are not lost... not exactly."

"Oh." She looked up, awaiting the large man's explanation.

"I guess you could say our friend is lost," Asar said. Turning to face Keith, he fished for assurance, nodding as he spoke. "And we have come here to find him... and bring him home."

"Home?" Azrael repeated. "Where is that?"

Keith laughed. "Not here."

"So anyway," Asar continued, "we are trying to find our friend and lend a hand, if necessary."

"I think you should leave... now." The little girl's face took on a shadowy hue.

"Really?" Keith couldn't take any more.

"Nope," Azrael said, laughing. "Just teasing... he told me to creep you out a bit."

"He?" Asar was confused.

"Yes!" Her laughter now verged on being uncontrollable. "Come on, I'll take you to him."

"Take us to whom, exactly?" Asar called out, trying to keep pace with Azrael, who was picking up her pace.

"Decks," she called back to them.

"Decker?" Keith smiled at Asar, then turned back to Azrael.

"Duhhh..." She took a sharp left between the outskirts of two separate resort properties, causing the two men to sprint to keep up. "Oh, and he said to tell you, *the big one...*"

"Yes?" Asar's speech was labored, as was his breathing.

"He said to tell you, you're late!"

15

Atticus took a long, deep drag from the cigarette clinging to the corner of his mouth. The glowing ash trail growing at the end gave way to gravity and fell into his lap, causing him to sit up in his chair cursing as he brushed the burnt remains away.

"Fuck."

Licking his fingers, he attempted to wash the black soot from his blue jeans with a bath of saliva. His aggravation grew as his efforts only caused the black traces to smear about his leg. "God damn... fucking shit!"

"What's wrong, love?" Jade asked as she strolled in from the bedroom of their renovated section of the castle in Craco, Italy. Her sultry movements, coupled with the sweet aroma of dark amber that encapsulated her being, drained Atticus of his angry fit instantaneously.

"Nothing, nothing... I'm fine." He smiled as she positioned herself in front of him in the chair, legs parted strongly with her hands on her hips. He looked up at her heavenly physique with her short, body-contouring skirt and devilishly high heels, and wondered how he had found her. Actually, that was a lie. Jade had found him, slaving away in that pathetic hole of an antiquities shop outside of Rome. She had struck up a conversation with him about the ancient Roman influences in Egypt during times of occupation. Her knowledge of early cultures, and, he learned on her third visit to the shop, her vast and dark knowledge of the occult, was awe inspiring. He was taken with her from day one, and when she began to tell stories of magic and the hidden troves of treasure that were scattered across the globe, he suggested they work together to investigate her claims. And she said yes! Within a days' time, he found himself in the ruined and abandoned Italian ghost town of Craco, making love and making plans. Plans not only to recover various ancient and sacred artifacts, but to use the power that would be derived from these acquisitions to rise and to dominate.

"Are you sure?" she purred, leaning down towards him.

"Yes, yes..." he said, smiling. "I got ash on my pants. Nothing... silliness..."

"Oh, you poor thing." She played with him, running her long nails down his thigh. "I think you should get them off."

Atticus laughed and attempted to rise from the chair, hands already working the buttons of his jeans, when he found himself pressed back into the seat by the palm of Jade's hand. "Easy there, cowboy," she smirked. "Have you finished reading the research I gave you?"

"Almost," he said, sounding winded already. "I'll finish it later... yes?" He attempted to stand once more, and she pushed him back again.

"No," she replied sharply, taking a step back.

"Look, look..." he pleaded. "I know where we go to already."

"You know where we are going," Jade replied, smirked again as she corrected his English.

"Yes." He stood, tapping the cover of the deteriorating leather book on the table beside him. "Yes, I know where... where we are going next."

"Good." Her voice was purring once more. "Enlighten me... talk to me."

"West Bank," he said, tapping the book again. "Qumran."

Atticus watched as she lifted her hand to her face and ran a finger across her lips, her eyes lost in deep thought. He waited silently as she pondered his assessment of the materials. Finally, her lips curved up and she smiled.

"The scrolls..." Jade began to walk back towards him.

"No."

His response stopped her in her tracks and a puzzled look formed on her brow. Her Asian-influenced eyes, dark and fiery all at once, stared at him for clarification.

He smiled excitedly. "One scroll in particular... a metal scroll."

"Ahhh." She smiled and resumed her dance towards her victim. "Would that metal be, say, copper in nature?" Jade teased as she pushed the shoulders of her dress off her arms, exposing the soft, tanned skin beneath.

"Yes." Atticus' voice trembled like a schoolboy at her display.

"Is something in the Copper Scroll's list of import to our journey?" She continued as her dress fell to the floor around her patent leather strappy black heels.

"Yes!" he almost found himself shouting. "Smart... bad girl."

Jade stepped forward, lifting her long, silky legs from the circle of dress below her. Her exquisite body, adorned with seductively-placed tattoos at her hips, thighs and ribs, stood before Atticus, and his limbs quivered as she planted her palms on his chest and shoved him down into the chair.

"Let me show you what a bad little girl I am," she whispered as she dropped to her knees before him, the curve of her rear wiggling in the air like an excited tail, as she reached for the zipper of his ash-stained pants.

16

The murky green water parted its fathomless darkness to the power of Jericho's light. Fighting the rash of undertow and conflicting currents, he pressed on in his descent into the lifeblood of the Egyptian civilization. The Nile, blessed with the grandeur of innumerable empires, swelled around his body and forced the impeccably fit diver to employ all of his muscles to meet the challenge of forward progress. Pressing on, Jericho began to lose track of spatial reality as speckled and dusted water gave way to nothing more than the same, and a feeling of non-movement wrestled at his senses.

"Shit." His words vocalized as muffled echoes in the churning waters. He tilted his head from side-to-side and attempted in desperation to focus the light in all directions. Jericho's eyes, encapsulated in a prison of rubber and glass, darted about hoping to catch a glimpse of some jutting edge of stone, or perhaps a long-forgotten vestige of one of the innumerable pantheons of sandstone gods that were sure to litter the bottom of the timeless river - a fish, a twig, anything, anything but the sea of desolate green that filled every corner of his vision.

"Shit." He gritted over his mouthpiece once more.

As thoughts of surfacing filled his mind with ever-growing intensity, his prayers in desperation were answered, and not a minute too soon, as his limbs had begun to ache and stiffen with the all-too-familiar pangs of exhaustion. Below and before him, the rough outlines of a stone edifice began to materialize, and the rugged and asymmetrical landscape became clearer as he grew closer. Pounding at the water around him to propel him to his target with newly found fervor, he came to rest at the stone's canopy within seconds. Grappling against the rock to stave off the current, Jericho allowed himself but a moment to recover from his descent and soon found himself working his way around what was clearly a man-made stone structure. His efforts soon gave way to an indentation of sufficient size for him to shift and shimmy his body into. Passing through the tunnel of rock, claustrophobic shivers began to traverse his spine and toy with his mind, a sense that was quite honestly foreign to the seasoned explorer. Perhaps it was the dark, all-consuming currents that enveloped him, or maybe the exhaustive maneuvers he had undertaken to reach this point - either way, he found himself teetering on the verge of panic.

Keep it together, he thought as he bit down hard on the rubber lifeline in his mouth, commanding compliance from his body and mind. *Straighten up and fly right.* The mantra filled his head and became a focal point. He kicked his flippers hard and shot through the streaming tunnel with the grace and speed of a dolphin.

"Straighten up..." Biting down hard, the submerged words which resounded in his head soon took on new acoustics as Jericho burst through the water's surface into open air. "Fly right!" he bellowed out into the echoing air, allowing his regulator to drop from his lips.

Finding a shelf of rock to stand on, he propped himself upright and out of the water. Raising his light, he traced the outlines of his surroundings and was more than exuberant at what his eyes found. The small cave-like temple was adorned with spectacular homages to the supreme queen of Egyptian deities, Isis. Stone statues, masterfully chiseled, lay scattered in all four corners of the submerged citadel. Jericho's illuminations bounced and danced across the surfaces of still more renditions of the mother of Horus, cast in the brilliance of what must surely be gold and silver, surprisingly untarnished and unmarred by the passage of time or the tropic-like moisture that filled the cavernous hideaway.

Having allowed himself a moment to soak in the splendor of his find, Jericho trotted forward on his flippers and hoisted himself completely up and out of the algae-laden water of the Nile that filled the center of the temple. Hobbling forward, not unlike a penguin in his movement, he crouched and rolled sideways on the hard stone below him and released his feet from the rubber swim aids. Springing up, Jericho allowed the soles of his feet to soak up the firm support of the rock floor beneath him.

"Terra firma," he muttered with amusement and relief to be solidly planted on the temple's ornately-tiled floor. Studying the chamber from his newly achieved vantage point, Frank quickly found what he was looking for: a finely carved, immense slab altar at the back and center of the temple. Jericho, with his beam of light focused straight ahead, strode across the ancient ground towards his objective. He did not grant himself the pleasure of examining all the art and treasure that surrounded him. Storm had been very specific on this topic. He was to be concerned only with the objective, and Alexander had told him – no, had ordered him - not to pay any heed to the rest of the temple. He had to ignore the statues, ignore the gold and treasure - even dwelling on the architecture could be detrimental. According to his benefactor, all the grandeur of the temple was nothing more than a ruse, and if one allowed oneself to stray too long on these items, one could quickly become trapped in a mental escapade of no return.

Arriving before the altar, Jericho was pleased to find only one object upon its surface and surmised his job had just gotten easier. He reached out and grasped the large ushabti statue with one hand and brought it close for examination. Ushabtis, or servant statutes, were quite common in an ancient Egyptian's funerary arsenal. The fabled figures carved in the likeness of the deceased were meant to act as servants in the afterlife. The dead's likeness would rise to the task of any demands for manual labor placed on the departed. A proper burial consisted of 365 ushabti statues, one for each day of the year. Whenever the dead individual was called upon to work the fields or labor over stone, he could send his replica statue to perform the task in his stead.

"Servant statue," Jericho informed himself as he studied the mummy-formed figure. Rotating the object in his hand, he studied the sides closely, looking for evidence of something more than a simple figurine.

"Gotcha," he exclaimed with a smile as he identified the faint traces of an indent line running all along the center of the ushabti. He placed the light on the altar and took the top and bottom halves of the figure securely in his grasp. Pulling strenuously in opposite directions, he finally felt the stone halves begin to give way.

SPLASH!

Jericho momentarily froze at the distinctive sound of a disturbance in the dark pool of water behind him. Regaining his composure, he secreted away the statue in his gear's pouch and snatched his light from the altar. Spinning slowly and training his beam on the surface of the water, Jericho took one step forward. There, at its center, he could still make out the receding remains of ripples running like an accordion to the rock-adorned shore of the cavern's pool. He hadn't imagined it. Something had disturbed the water. Perhaps a piece of falling debris, or even a drop, albeit a large one, of Nile water had fallen from the ceiling. The scourge of the Nile's currents were swelling right overhead after all. Perhaps a bucket's worth of H2O had wormed its way through the stone and plummeted to the pool.

Yeah, that was probably it, he assured himself. Could've even been an accumulation of moisture that, much like a rain cloud, must eventually heed gravity's command.

"Doesn't matter," he advised the darkness. *I got what I came for. Time to hightail it outta here.*

No longer hesitating on the mystery of the splash, Jericho tapped the prize in his vest and took a step towards the pool and the route of his ultimate escape from the stone tomb. It was then that he saw it, the first of them, slowly emerge from the green, dark depths of the Nile. A pair of tell-tale nostrils, followed by a prehistoric-like snout and tangled fangs. It had risen from the water so slowly, so effortlessly, that the surface bore no signs of disturbance. Jericho stared in silent terror. Shifting his stance slightly, he slowly lifted his right leg to retrace his step backwards, away from the dangers of the water. It was then, leg in mid-air, that he saw the second pair of nostrils, snout, and teeth bob to the surface.

"As if..." he whispered, fear in his voice. "As if one crocodile wasn't enough."

Frank's words were met with sour dismay as his weary eyes watched the scene repeat itself four more times and he found himself staring into a pool of six Nile crocodiles.

17

Azrael, Asar, and Keith moved side by side through the streets of the urban wasteland. The forgotten Tunisian city's roadways had all but returned to dirt, and dust clouds kicked up in their wake as Asar and Keith struggled to keep pace with their peculiar little guide.

"Just ahead." Azrael's voice was musical and bore no signs of fatigue. "Decks is right ahead."

"Very good," Asar huffed. "Is he safe?" The labored words exited his mouth listlessly, and Azrael came to a sudden halt.

"Are you okay?" She turned and reached out, taking hold of the old battle horse's hand.

A giggle escaped the towering fortress that was Asar, and he smiled reluctantly at the small girl. "Quite fine, my dear... quite fine."

"He's fine," Keith interjected. "Just getting older, that's all," he added with a smirk.

"We all are." Azrael released Asar's hand and pivoted in Keith's direction. The suddenly focused, adult expression on the girl's face took Keith aback, and he stumbled to reply to her philosophical retort.

"Yeah." A strained smile retracted his facial muscles. "Yeah, I guess you're right."

"So best get a move on," Azrael blurted out and proceeded to hop-to at a soldier's pace, sprinting towards the ruins of the once lavish hotel that stretched to the sky before them. Asar and Keith exchanged amused glances and fell in behind their little leader. It was just like Decker to procure the favor and friendship of a native inhabitant. He had a way of assimilating quite effortlessly into the community and culture of his locale. Years of non-stop travel had made this trait a requirement for both his physical well-being - and his sanity.

Azrael rested before the tattered and broken entryway of the deserted resort. She called out to the duo. "Come on, slow pokes!"

The two said nothing in response and continued their cautious approach to the towering carcass of a hotel. Keith watched as the young girl shrugged and disappeared into the darkness beyond the building's threshold.

"She's gone!" he shouted, alerting Asar of their guide's departure from view. "You sure this is cool? Not a trap, right? I don't feel like walking into a zombie apocalypse, man."

"Quite sure." Asar all but disregarded Keith's juvenile discourse.

The pair trudged on through the sweltering, unabashed heat of the midday sun as it beat down upon them.

"Like, *really* sure?"

"Look." Asar practically skidded to a halt and directed his companion's attention to the far side of the expansive circular entrance drive, which was surely once a brilliant undertaking of masonry. Squinting to repel the rays of the sun, Keith could make out the distinctive features of a vehicle in the distance.

"William's Jeep," Asar announced for Keith's benefit, just in case he wasn't adding one and one and getting two. "He's in there," he assured his weary companion as they resumed their approach.

"Care to fill me in a little, Asar?" Keith thought it was an appropriate question at this particular point in their journey. He had purposefully kept many of his questions at bay until now, sensing his companion's reluctance to share too much with him. He assumed, and rightly so, that the Egyptian was more concerned with Keith's apprehension and fear than in keeping the details of their mission for Storm from him. Asar had chosen to go dark on him more for Keith's own peace of mind than anything else, and the sentiment had not been lost on him. Keith sensed, however, that they were fast approaching the apex of their task and he deserved to be apprised of the situation at hand.

"We're here to secure William's safe passage home, Keith," he offered, not missing a beat or a step in their forward progress. "Nothing more... nothing less."

"Really?" Keith's skepticism clung to his words. "And Zorha's satchel? The item she gave you?"

"A key to a lock." Asar's tone was serious. "A key to a lock, and nothing more."

The shattered frame of the hotel's entrance was only a few steps from them now, and Keith longed for the shade of the abandoned building's interior.

"And what about the madness on the train?" Keith blurted out, abruptly spinning around in front of Asar and blocking his path forward. "What about the supernatural freak show? And the attack in the cab?"

Asar moved with unexpected agility sharply and was soon past Keith, who was left staring ahead at the route they had just come from.

"Impediments, my dear boy," Asar called out. "Just like you are being right now... an impediment to William's safe passage home."

Keith jogged to his side and shook his head. "Really?" he said, with annoyance clinging to his words. "There's nothing I need to know?"

Asar stopped and looked down at his companion. "William is inside... he is being held against his will. By whom or what, I do not yet know. Zorha's satchel is the ransom, if you will, which was demanded for William's release. With all sincerity, I do not know much more beyond that, my boy."

"Okay," Keith nodded.

"Okay." Asar winked and turned, stepping over the shards of glass and debris at his feet before disappearing into the refuge of the building's darkness.

18

Jade purred down the Jordanian road in the heart of the city of Amman with such confidence that everyone she passed suddenly paused from their market-haggling and village-gossiping to gaze upon her movements. Although shrouded in folds of linen, her presence and goddess-like physique were evident. She carried her tall frame through the sand-bitten vendors and tattered patrons with a focus that all but drowned out the din of the busy Arab city. Her movements pulled the cloth of her guise to and fro, causing each sway to capture taut linen against one part of her body or another, allowing gawkers the momentary thrill of her hidden feminine curves. She marched with purpose towards the heart of the metropolis. At its center lay the new Jordan Museum, and at the museum's center lay her objective.

The Ras Al-Ein district of Amman was a mixture of market stands and homes. The museum was subterranean to an elevated, graduated segment of land above which was littered with buildings at its highest point. Below that area lay a sea of small homes which overshadowed the sprawling museum at the land gradient's lowest point. The museum, built in 2014 and financed through governmental grants and loyal Jordanian patrons, was crafted in the ancient mastaba, or step style, and was an architectural attraction in and of itself.

"Just ahead," she hissed to Atticus, who remained a step or two behind. Jade's long legs carried her in an otherworldly fashion, and a double step was required to keep pace.

"I see it," the magician panted, pumping his legs in overtime. "The plan? What's the plan sweetheart? You said you would fill me in."

"Let us arrive first," she whispered. "I need to apprise the situation. However, the plan is simple in its ultimate goal: secure the scroll."

Atticus caught up with her just as they landed at the base of the museum steps. She paused and turned to him. His face was red, and a sheen of sweat painted his features in an unattractive way that made Jade grimace.

"You have to cut back on the burgers, my dear," she said, laughing.

Atticus gulped a deep breath. "I'm fine... cut the crap, okay?"

"Touchy touchy..." Jade reached out and tickled under his chin as if consoling a moody feline.

Atticus swiped at her hand, smacking it to the side. Jade opened her eyes wide in response.

"I said cut the crap!" he chided, and climbed the steps ahead of her.

"All right, all right." She laughed, trotting to his side. "I was kidding. Don't get your panties in a bunch."

Atticus came to an abrupt halt at the entrance to the museum and turned to face Jade, who was now right behind him. Reaching out, he took hold of both her arms and pressed them to her side, essentially trapping her in place.

"You brute," she whispered with a smile.

"You better cut the shit, Jade," he said, grinding his teeth together. "Or I'm gonna bunch your fucking panties up. You don't know when to give it a rest."

Jade, sensing the end of her amusement, pouted at her annoyed companion. "I'm engaged in folly," she pleaded. "Joking to pass the time."

Atticus, recognizing his overreaction, immediately released his diminutive assistant's arms and took a step back.

"Look." His voice was even now. "You are so hot," he said, smiling. "And when you make fun of me like that, I think I'm not good enough for you, okay? So zip it, will ya?"

Jade shook her head and walked past the insecure magician. "Okay," she whispered. "Now that we've shared our feelings, can we get on with it?"

He nodded in response. "Sure... what's the plan?"

"For fuck's sake!" she belted out. "We need to find Dr. Awain."

"A friend of yours?" Atticus asked as the two passed through the threshold and into the museum.

"Not likely," she offered with a snicker. "He has something I want."

"What's that?"

"The keys to the castle."

19

Jericho rubbed his forehead between his thumb and pointer finger, rolling his hand over his dark skin several times in an effort to fend off the migraine that was beginning to take root.

"What the hell... what the hell?" he mumbled to himself, raising his eyes and the light to the pool of water. The enormous Nile reptiles were still there.

Silent. Waiting. Waiting for him.

Surely this was no coincidence. They were on a mission – no doubt some directive of the old gods who clearly intended on stopping Jericho from leaving with the ancient artifact. The beasts floated just below the water's surface, motionless.

Okay, he thought, perking up a bit. *Not about to become a relic in this tomb.* Circling around with the light, he stopped on several sets of hieroglyphics carved directly into the stone wall beside him. He studied the archaic strokes for a moment and whispered, "...and I know for shit-sure that doesn't say, *here lies Frank mutha-fuckin' Jericho.*" Smiling, he quickly shook off his growing feelings of despair.

My fate's not written in stone. Time to change it up.

Jericho took a more detailed survey of his surroundings. The power of his light was not endless - he needed to make the most of what time he had left in the battery.

"Gotta be another way outta here," he whispered to one of the stoic stone statues of Isis that littered the tomb. "Any chance you want to point the way, sweetheart?"

Without further hesitation, he vaulted atop the stone altar and directed his light on the ceiling above. There was nothing but rock and the hum of the flowing river on the other side. Hopping down, he moved quietly about the chamber, checking every edifice, nook, or indent he came across. This place was solid, and he knew it. It had survived the annual rise and fall of the Nile - biting over its surface for thousands of years. The passage of time stood as a testament to the submerged enclosure's fortitude, but it was also this very notion that afforded Jericho a sliver of hope. There must be a chink in the tomb's structural armor somewhere. He just needed to find it without alerting the crocs to his movement in the process.

Jericho shined his light on the scaly monsters again. Checking to ensure they were not on the move, he found them in relatively the same position he had left them. Pivoting to study the floor of the chamber a little closer, he had not completely turned from the water when the slightest of surface ripples caught his eye. Stretching his head toward the water ever so slowly, Jericho squinted to confirm that something had disturbed the pool. He watched as the last remnants of the echo of water came to an end over the shoreline of stone at his feet.

Crouching down to the water's edge, he positioned himself and waited.

DRIP

There it was again. Not much, but a drip from above, all the same. Perhaps the source of the falling water would prove to be a weak spot in the ceiling of his stone prison. Perhaps it was a way out. Or perhaps there were more crocs waiting above.

Ahhh, shit. His lips went through the motions, but not a sound escaped his mouth.

DRIP... DRIP

There it was again - a double shot. He swiftly trained his light on the rocks above the pool of water. There – he saw the faintest glimmer of moisture. He studied the rock, which quickly began to visually blend together in the dim light. Squinting for some imaginary advantage, he waited and was soon rewarded with the formation and eventual drop of what could become his liquid cell key. A sliver of hope ran down the seasoned explorer's spine as he stretched forward with robot-like movements. Using the artifacts and stone as a makeshift ladder, he slowly made his way to the surface of the ceiling. Retrieving his light from his belt, he studied the area and was rendered breathless by what he found. The pooling and dripping Nile water was seeping through at the center of a perfectly straight cut in the stone. The chiseled and obviously man-made line in the rock was about six feet long, give or take a few inches, and ended on either side with an intersecting cut forming a capital "I" at the roof of the tomb.

It was a passage. There was no doubt. Excitement, and possibly salvation, stirred in Jericho's aching bones.

"Now just need to find the..." Frank's whispers trailed off to silence as his light came to rest on an odd-shaped relief that was centered and offset from the passage line. "Trigger."

His words echoed through the chamber, and he quickly realized he overstepped the boundary of his orations. Turning his beam, to his dismay he found the dinosaur-like lizards on the move. Having exited the pool already, the cluster of dreary scales had begun to scale the rocks and walls of the tomb with unnatural agility. At their current pace they would be on him in seconds. He scurried across the rocks below his feet and dropped to his knees. Leaning upside-down, he reached for the peculiar relief of the wings of Isis he had noticed on the ceiling. Instead of the outstretched customary depiction of Isis's wings, this rendering had them folded at her side. It was a one-in-a-million shot based on a one-in-a-million hunch. Without looking back at the progress of the beasts, he grasped the stone wings with both hands and yanked them free from their ancient dust, extending them out. The last thing Jericho saw was the open and rancid jaws of the largest croc lunging at him before an onslaught of Nile water drove everything down.

20

"Dr. Awain," Jade said to the guard, pouting. "Be a dear and point us in his direction."

The rigidly fit guard glared at her with obvious disdain. His eyes disapproved of her attire, and his grimaced lips disapproved of her flirtatious nature.

"And you are?" he asked, looking past her to apprise her companion. His disapproval was even more evident now.

She laughed, turning to Atticus for the theatrics of it. "I? Well, I am... I."

The guard returned his attentions to Jade. "The doctor has no time for unannounced meetings with tourists," he said, beginning to turn his back on the pair. "Be on your way."

Jade stepped into his body's circular motion, with her face very close to his. "Pick up that phone and call the good doctor. Let him know Professor Atticus and his assistant from America are here and require an immediate audience."

She paused, studying the cogs rotating behind the sentry's eyes.

"Do it," she hissed. "Do it now."

Without further contestation, the soldier grabbed the phone on the desk behind him. Jade listened as the man spoke in muffled

Arabic, catching most of his conversation. She turned and winked at Atticus playfully.

"The doctor wants to know what this is in regard to," the soldier asked, covering the mouthpiece of the antiquated telephonic equipment.

Jade smiled. "Oh my, he doesn't remember." She moved closer to the watchman again, her voice now serious and convincing. "We are here to do the bio-piece on Dr. Awain for the huge spread on his work in the American Journal of Archaeology. Surely, he recalls our letters and emails."

The guard relayed the message and Jade could hear shouting on the other end. She quickly saw signs of reprimand creep across the poor sap's face.

"The doctor will be right up to greet you," the guard said, his tone and demeanor transformed in the blink of an eye. "Please have a seat over here." He directed them to some couches. "A refreshment? Anything, please instruct me."

"That will be all, soldier," Jade said, laughing, and walked past him, running a finger across his broad shoulder as she passed. "You have been most helpful."

21

Asar was delighted to find Azrael just inside the entrance of the crumbling vestiges of the resort. He smiled and nodded as if to say, *I had no doubt you would be with us.*

"There you are!" shouted Keith as he animatedly stepped to the young girl's side. "I was afraid you ditched us."

Azrael laughed. "Were you afraid?"

"That's not what I meant," he said, rebuffing her teasing. "I was worried for you."

"Ha," Asar chimed in. "The young lady has survived in this apocalypse for some time, Keith."

"What's the plan?" Keith asked. He did not feel like being the brunt of anyone's ribbing and ignored them both. "Can I be enlightened now, please?"

Asar paused and turned to his companion. "Keith, I am not keeping you in the dark, son. I have already given you all the pertinent information." His words trailed off a bit as he surveyed their dimly lit surroundings. "Sorry to say, but I myself am in the dark, as it were..." He waved his arms about at their dank quarters. "...as to what comes next."

"What?" Keith exclaimed. "What is with you and Storm? You both constantly act like you have everything under control and in hand. But that's clearly not the case. It never is. So why not just drop the charade, Asar?"

Asar was well aware that Keith's sudden burst of aggression was primarily fueled by fear, so he did his best to keep matters in perspective while formulating a response.

Reaching out and placing a hand on the young man's shoulder, he spoke softly and sincerely. "Perhaps it is because the illusion of order is in the best interests of all involved. Anything else would serve no benefit other than escalating fear and eventually spreading mutiny. If, however, dear Keith, you wish to be privy to all knowledge of our *quests*, for lack of a better word, than I shall be sure to apprise you of every detail, danger, possible outcome and, for that matter, the likelihood of us surviving said outcome. This is what I shall do going forward. Does this approach suit you?"

Keith stared at Asar as ignorant confusion swelled in his eyes. He flashed a glance at Azrael who was grimacing at him, apparently also awaiting a response.

"No," he finally piped up, shaking his head gently. "No, I don't suppose that would be very productive."

"Well, that's settled." Asar slapped him on the back endearingly. "Shall we?"

"Wait." Keith grabbed his arm. "Wait, there must be a happy middle ground. Keeping someone too far out of the loop can also generate apprehension and," he said, turning to Azrael, "fear."

The little girl giggled at what she chalked up to his silliness and smiled with familiarity at her new companion.

"Agreed," said Asar. He moved past Keith, progressing further into the dilapidated ruins of the massive hotel.

"Hey," Azrael called from behind him. "That was fun!" she said, laughing. "Now *I* have something to share."

Keith felt his blood run cold. If asked, he wouldn't be able to explain where the feeling came from. But it came. Was it her phrasing? Was it her slightly-morphed features, which were possibly nothing more than an optical illusion brought about by the poor lighting, speckled and distorted by floating showers of dust and ruinous puffs of microscopic debris? Or perhaps it was simply her improperly placed jovial demeanor in the heart of this palatable dreariness.

"Well, let's have it girl," Asar demanded roughly. Keith sensed the hulking Egyptian had caught wind of the same apprehension that was swirling around him.

"William sent me," she said, her voice losing all traces of lightheartedness. "Shall I take you to him?"

22

Alexander paced the floor up and down the length of the behemoth wooden table in the castle's dining room. He was awaiting the tardy arrival of his misfit assemblage for a mandatory meeting of minds. He toyed with the "misfit" label that had popped into his thoughts and how it really was an unfair title conjured by a weary head. He had grown fond of each and every one of them, even Samantha. Especially Samantha. Her mere presence had acted like a magnet against his steely friend Lobo. And she, in turn, had been drawn to him.

Alexander mused internally at the true test, sappy as it were, of his fellowship's strength and worth. Simply put, he could not imagine facing whatever the future held without them by his side. His mysterious roots wound back through time, and he and his ancestors before had been tasked with maintaining order and balance between the spheres of darkness and light. The task had proven, for all intents and purposes, to be a mostly solitary venture. Sure, he had the likes of Asar and Serket, and others of their caliber through the millennia, to extend that helping hand when it was called for. But he had never been blessed with the likes of the group he now referred to as The Dragon Storm. The whole premise of having others to lean on, to depend on, was entirely foreign to him, and he was doing his best to become accustomed to this new chapter in his existence.

It was altogether thrilling and frightening all at once.

For while he was energized by their assistance and the ability to delegate tasks and accomplish more, quicker, he was also faced with the constant fear for their safety. Would he entrust one of them with a task that was beyond their abilities? Would he open the mental flood gates of another and inundate them with knowledge which encapsulated more than they could handle? These questions and apprehensions plagued his waking hours and haunted his dreams.

Alex's thoughts were severed as Philip shuffled in through the kitchen entrance and past his old friend. "They will be down shortly, Alexander. Relax and let me pour you a drink." He spoke without looking at Storm, as if he needed no visual confirmations of his employer's state.

"I do not want a drink, Philip." The words came out with a spit of hostility. "I want people to be reliable and adhere to my requests."

Philip stopped fidgeting around the table and peered up at Alexander, who was already nodding his head in acknowledgment.

"Sorry old man," Alex said. He took a deep breath and hopped in a chair at the head of the table. "How about that drink then, while we... wait."

"Ha!" Philip snickered and withdrew a small bottle of bourbon from somewhere within his jacket. Grasping the cork between his teeth, he yanked it free like a salty pirate and grabbed one of the coffee mugs from the center of the table. Wiping imaginary dust from the ceramic with the bottom edge of his coat, he placed the cup down and poured Alexander a full glass.

"What," Alex jested, "no spit shine?"

"Shut up, you old fool," Philip mumbled, smiling. Suddenly the main door flew open to the sound of the chatters of the rest of the castle's guests.

"I do cherish these warm moments together, Philip," Alexander rose to meet his crew. "Let's do it again soon, shall we?"

"Haaa." The stately caretaker huffed at the sarcasm, as Storm rose and rushed to greet the others. Peering down at the mug in his hand, Philip shrugged and downed the fine vintage in one gulp. Sleeving the residue from his lips, he turned to face the others, ushering them around the table.

"Come in, come in... sit," he commanded over the din of greetings and salutations. "Come out of the door... sit."

"Samantha!" Storm made it a point to greet her first, and she returned a forced, albeit sufficient for the time being, smile in response. "Your travels were adequate, I hope?"

"Everything was fine," she said, nodding. "All good."

"All good?" Alex perked up at the possibility of a double meaning in her words.

"What?" She shook her head. "Let's not push it, okay, big guy? I literally just walked in."

Although not the response he had hoped for, Alexander smiled nonetheless. It was better than silence, which is all he had received from Sam for months on end. He was more than happy to endure a little taste of her wise-ass quips. It was something. It was a start.

"Come please," Alex said, gesturing to Samantha and the others to join him at the table. "Let us not agitate Philip. By now, you are all well aware of how he gets."

"I think he's a dear," Kate called out as she climbed on her chair. "A castle treasure."

At this, Philip stopped dead in his tracks and practically whispered, "Thank you, Ms. Kate," before blushing and exiting the room.

Kate, shocked by his response, turned to Sam and rolled her eyes in ignorant playfulness, and they both broke out into giggles.

"Well," Alexander piped up, "it appears that after decades of not knowing how to dispatch the old fox, a compliment from Kate is the secret weapon." He allowed a sour smile to creep across his face, but quickly withdrew it as his eyes met Serket's. She recognized that face - the concern woven in his brow - and raised one eyebrow as a sign of recognition. Alex blinked once and nodded, returning his attention to the others.

"Please, please..." he said, ushering them into the seats around the table. "We all have some catching up to do, so let's get the business at hand resolved so that we may get on with the evening."

The restless chatter subsided as Alexander took his seat, jerking his hips forward. The antique wood of the chair scraped out a catcall as he slid himself in. Its sharp noise was sufficient to silence the others, and their eyes and ears now trained on their host.

"It pains me," he began, "to have to conduct a discussion of this nature on the heels of what transpired just a few months ago." He paused to solidify his regret. "But evil does not rest... so we in turn must remain vigilant. I have just returned from visits to France and Nova Scotia, and I am quite troubled by the results of my reconnaissance."

A serious fire burned behind Alexander's eyes as he described his foray in Paris at the theater and the subsequent atmospheric disturbance which leveled DeMolay's bookshop.

"What does it all mean?" asked Kate. The young woman being the first to inquire was something Storm was now accustomed to.

"Well, I have had the expanse of the time of my return to the castle to analyze and ponder both episodes, and to begin with, I believe they are certainly connected."

"How's that?" Sam uttered nonchalantly, clearly not wishing to convey any real signs of interest to Storm.

"I shall expound, Samantha," Alex said, addressing her directly, to which she rolled her eyes in Kate's direction. She wasn't sure if he had caught the gesture. She kind of hoped he had.

"The magician and his assistant called forth a very specific, very powerful demonic entity. I am sure of it. I glimpsed its figure beneath the cloth, and I identified the sigil burnt into the stage, a branding if you will - Essentially announcing Asmodeus was here."

Serket shifted in her seat at the sound of demon's name. Kate noted that she was clearly made uncomfortable by the mere utterance.

"As I said," Alex continued, "Asmodeus is no low-level demonic flunky. He is a powerful commander of Hell, and he is not one to be trifled with or bossed around by a simple purveyor of prestidigitation. This is something far more than smoke and mirrors, my friends. Atticus the Great is not so great as to be able to conjure and control a demon of this caliber without some assistance. I know of no incantation, no ancient grimoire, or compendium of spells that can call forth this prince of oblivion and command said entity. There is but one way to accomplish this feat. And that, my dear friends, is the infamous Ring of Solomon."

"The what?" asked Sam. She was on her knees in her seat now, no longer working very hard at masking her intrigue.

"Solomon's Ring," Serket repeated, never breaking her glance, which was locked on Alexander.

"It's the legendary ring King Solomon used to command the demons of Hell, given to him by an angel," Kate said. She now took a turn at illuminating Samantha. "Or by God himself."

"Why would God give this King Solomon a ring to control demons?" Samantha asked the room. "Why not a ring to destroy them or something?"

"A very good question, Samantha." Alex used the moment to

encourage his most difficult ward's involvement. "A good question, indeed."

He peered across the table at the others. "Anyone?" he prodded.

"Construction!" Kate smiled and winked at Storm.

"Construction," he repeated, slowly emphasizing the word as to convey her correctness.

"Huh?" Sam said, slumping back in her seat.

"They are teasing, Samantha." Serket reached over and touched her arm. "Well, sort of. What they mean is, Solomon used the ring to command that the demons construct the new temple. The Temple of Solomon. A massive undertaking." Her eyes grew wide at the thought.

"The assemblage of the gargantuan stones, as well as the speed at which the temple was erected, could only have been achieved with the assistance of Asmodeus and his legions of Hell."

"So, this magician..." Kate started.

"Atticus the Great." Alexander spit the name from his lips with disdain.

"Atticus the Great," Kate repeated. "He has King Solomon's Ring?"

Bowing his head slightly, Alexander nodded in the affirmative. "Yes Kate, I believe he does."

Silence filled the room. At this point, the severity of this premise had firmly taken root in everyone, even Samantha. Alexander leaned forward and scanned the table for the cup Philip had poured for him. It was nowhere to be found. Opening his mouth to speak again, he was cut short by an image on one of the covers of the several newspapers scattered about the massive tabletop. Philip had a habit of leaving several random copies of the day's paper, from different locals and in different languages, on the table for Alexander's review. Tilting his head slightly, he could make out some text and ascertained it was an Egyptian daily, most likely a few days old.

"What's the connection to the bookstore?" Samantha asked, breaking Alex's concentration. He looked up at her with a bit of a blank stare.

Recognizing his momentary detachment from the conversation, she inquired as to the cause of his distraction.

"Nothing, nothing..." Alexander replied. "You were saying?"

"Yeah..." Samantha leaned forward, side-eyeing the newsprint in front of her. She asked again. "What's the connection to DeMolay's shop?"

Alexander cleared his throat. "Well, if you recall, DeMolay was a Templar, and the Templar were entrusted, or rather, had granted themselves a self-imposed responsibility to guard the Ring of Solomon, as well as other items that are more commonly referred to as the *Temple Treasures*."

Storm tersely sprang to his feet, sliding his chair back as his body ascended away from the table. "I searched the shop before it was destroyed and located what I believe was the storage box that had housed it," he said, sighing with palpable concern. "However, the ring was not inside. Gone. On the finger of Atticus the Great, one must assume."

Alexander rounded the table towards Serket's side. His eyes were drawn to the scattered papers once more.

"And what about that very deliberate tornado you described?

Where does that fall in all this?" demanded Kate. She was on her feet now, trailing behind Alexander. "Do you think *that* was Asmodeus? Or something else under Atticus' command?"

"Not quite," said Alex. He turned abruptly, and Kate almost ran into him. "More likely a product of the real commander here... whomever is in charge of whatever is brewing."

Kate shrugged and looked to the others. She wanted to make sure she wasn't the only one not following. Their vacant stares were sufficient to set her mind at ease.

"I don't believe Atticus is necessarily pulling the strings," Alex continued. "The proverbial puppeteer of ancient demonic powers, he is not."

"What?" Sam said, snickering.

Serket noted Storm's speech patterns and realized his mind had left the room, or at least, had broken company from the three of them. "Hey," she whispered loudly, "care to finish that thought?"

Alex darted forward, reached out across the center of the table, and snatched the newspaper which had become the focal point of his attentions. Drawing it to his face, he began to read silently. After a momentary pause, he lowered the paper.

"I have only experienced a weather pattern similar to what I encountered recently once before. And this fact triggers grave concern in me, because the purveyor of the cyclonic wind display from the past should no longer be among us."

"Whoa, cowboy..." Samantha was on her feet now as well, attempting to make her way around the table to join the others. "You want to gimme that again?"

"No," Alexander replied curtly, dropping the newspaper to the floor and cutting a bee line to the door. Kate bent down to retrieve the scattered sheets and glanced at the headline with burning curiosity, mouthing the words as she read.

"*Five ancient silver swords uncovered in the recesses of Dead Sea cave.*"

Serket attempted to wrangle Alexander as he passed, to no avail.

"Wait!" she exclaimed, "where are you going?"

"And what does this mean?" Kate exclaimed, holding the now crumpled newsprint in the air.

"I am going to arrange a date with a demon," he answered without missing a stride. "And that, my dear Kate," he said, referring to the Egyptian News in her hand, "is yet another example of why I do not subscribe to the irrational premise of coincidence."

23

Frank Jericho broke the surface of the cold blackness that was the Nile and sucked air into his burning lungs like a four-barrel carburetor in a '69 Chevelle SS: in big bursting gulps. Squinting at the bright moon which had been his only guide through the opening in the top of the temple, he allowed a smile to cross his lips.

"Thanks buddy," he whispered to the celestial orb, and began to pivot in the water to get his bearings. He had no doubt that if he was able to find his way out of the temple ruins, the massive reptiles wouldn't be far behind. And unlike him, their eyes worked just fine submerged in dark water. He was a sitting duck - or better yet, a sitting Jericho. Or even better, a doggy-paddling Jericho.

"Oh man," he huffed. The humor just kept coming. He didn't care. He was hopped up on adrenaline and he had made it to the surface alive, prize in hand. It was becoming an all-too familiar feeling, and he was most definitely acquiring an addiction to that rush. It was no surprise that his euphoria was best achieved on one of Storm's errands. He always seemed to present the most danger for the smallest reward. But heck, it was Storm. He owed the guy ten times over, so the shit would continue to hit that fan for some time - that is, unless the moon would fail to guide him to safety, or the necessary bottom would drop out. Otherwise, he would continue to traipse around the globe whenever he was asked for, as often as it was required. Done deal. No need to ponder it. He needed to make the shore, and there was his next life buoy... his guide Aptera's shimmering flashlight. The items he had recovered were safely in a water bag with its string pulled tight to cinch it shut. He placed the string between his teeth, allowing the bag to trail back in the water around his shoulder, and started the difficult swim against the amazingly powerful current of the river.

"Fuck!"

The words escaped his lips, but the bag's string did not. Something rough had whipped across his leg - or had he whipped his leg across something rough? Either way, it didn't matter now. There was zero fight in his position. No visual, no protection or cover, no weapon. He was at the mercy of the ancient gods, and he was either going to make it to the dry sand of the Nile shore, or he was going to be a lizard's dinner. It was no longer his call, and he resigned himself to this. Calm controlled him. Pushing on, he found the light of the guide's beacon growing larger. He was almost there.

Just push it out, Frank, he thought. Or maybe he spoke again through his gritted, string holding teeth. Again, he didn't care.

Twenty seconds away.

His eyes bulged in the darkness. He had not swiped, he had *been* swiped, and much harder this time. He felt the warm burn on his calf. Whatever it was had opened him up, and he was now leaking blood into the murky depths of the Nile. He might as well fire a flare gun and spray lizard hormone all over himself.

Ten seconds.

A few more strokes and he was there. The beautiful image of Aptera was as clear as day - he was that close.

Five seconds from shore.

Frank Jericho stopped dead in the water.

His body hung horizontal across the surface, with his mouth and part of his nose below water. He stared motionless. He was frozen.

There was no doubt about it. No superman shit here. Nose-to-nose, a mere inch from his face was the snout of the biggest, baddest croc he had ever seen. The moon bounced across the beast's eyes, a silver shimmer amplified transversely on the black-filled lens of its pupil.

Silent. Motionless.

The creature stared into Frank, and Frank stared back into the creature.

Time ticked away by seconds up to eternity, and the movement of the water seemed to cease in the area around the two bodies. The guide was yelling now. Frank couldn't make it out, but either Aptera saw the croc and was warning him, or he didn't see it and was simply telling him to get out of the river. Either way didn't matter. He was staying where he was. Wasn't moving a muscle.

The exchange continued for at least a minute, maybe two. It really did feel much longer to Frank. He was beginning to lose hope. He had become sure the monster was a guardian of the temple he had just burglarized and then destroyed, and that it was savoring his fear until it would devour him.

Then the gosh-darn strangest thing happened. The majestic crocodile slowly submerged and disappeared. All traces were gone. No ripples or movement in the water. Gone. For whatever reason, it had granted Frank Jericho the right to exit the sacred river and carry on with his life. Jericho recognized the life-changing event that had just occurred, and promised himself to reflect on it more once he was safely in the air to New York.

Heaving himself hard, he clamored out and onto the sandy shore. Taking another engine intake's worth of air, he worked the muscles in his legs and rose upright. Releasing the bag from his teeth to his hand, he leaned sideways and examined the gash in his leg. It was a big ol' bad hole, but by some miracle, the bleeding had ceased. The magic water of the river, perhaps? Either way, it was time to get a move on.

Rising upright, he was taken by surprise to find the barrel of Aptera's gun almost as close to his face as the crocodile had just been.

"Fuck me," he spat as he slid the water bag's string over his head to hang about his neck and free his hands.

"Give to me," the guide demanded, pumping the large caliber revolver in and out in his direction. "Give me what you have removed from the temple."

Jericho hesitated. "Look," he started, "do you know what I just went through? I call time-out."

"What?" the Egyptian native demanded, not understanding. "Give me the bag or I will shoot you and take it off your corpse!"

"Corpse?" Frank murmured, not the vocab of a poverty-stricken village guide. Not at all.

"Who the hell are you?" Frank demanded.

The guide appeared to have had enough conversation and he leveled the weapon almost point blank at Frank's head.

"Bag... now... last chance." His native accent was gone, and a polished British accent replaced it. Jericho's shock was visible, and now he was really curious.

"I'm with Storm," Frank blurted out. "I work for Alexander Storm."

The guide's face relaxed a barely visible fraction and he smirked. "We know who you are, Francis. We know all about you."

"This is getting funky, man." Jericho began to plea anew, but to no avail.

"Enough!"

A powerful barrel of light stretched out from the desert night to their rear. Shining on Frank and his captor, loud yells began to emanate from the direction of the light's origin. The guide turned slightly to appraise the situation, and Frank Jericho took his opening, moving like a bat out of hell back into the dark, churning, Nile.

Bending and arching his muscular dark body down, he created a powerful dive and disappeared into the shelter of the midnight water. He could feel the compression bolts of bullets breaking the surface around him and coming to a quick stop shortly after entering the river. The guide was firing blindly and really had no chance of hitting him while he was under the water.

Regaining his sharp senses, he pointed himself in the direction of the opposite shore and fired off a few powerful underwater strokes which helped propel him double the distance the current would have taken him alone. Fairly sure he was a safe enough distance away, he broke the surface of the water for the last time that night and gobbled up huge breaths of oxygen. Keeping just his nostrils above the waterline, he kicked his feet and continued to propel to the safe shoreline.

"You will never get out of Egypt alive, Frank Jericho!" The guide was yelling now at the top of his lungs, and the words hit home. *How the hell am I gonna get out of the desert safely, let alone the country?*

Jesus Christ. His head bobbed instinctively as the guide fired a few more random shots in his general direction. He was too far now, and the light was too dim - even more dim since a patch of clouds had decided to take a rest in front of the white face of the moon. He was safe... for now.

24

"A rather inopportune time, Alexander," Asar said, as he shielded his cell phone slightly with his large, sun-drenched hand.

Asar had scurried to the corner of the dilapidated entry hall to speak with some modicum of privacy. He was quite sure that the little girl, currently smiling at him through the dust-laden sunrays filtering into the space between them, was not a spy for the enemy. He had, however, learned to exercise an inordinate amount of caution, and now would be no different.

"I need but a moment," Alexander spoke over him, curtly. "Surely you can entertain such?"

Scanning the passage, Asar took in the sights and sounds of what lay ahead. He heard the creak of the crumbling structure, with its peeling and shattered walls. The putrefied smell of rot and mold lay so heavy in the air, he was sure it was almost a visible presence.

"Honestly Alexander, I really do not have a moment."

"What of William?" Alex continued paying no mind to Asar's objections.

"We are..." he stuttered. "That is what I am trying to tell you. We are several footsteps from his location, and I would like very much to effectuate this exchange and be on our way. And by 'away,' I mean away from this entire God-forsaken place."

"All right... all right, old friend." Alex could hear the near panic in Asar's voice, and an unintended jovial snicker followed his words as a vision of the monstrous man harried and worried played out in his mind's eye. "I will let you carry on."

"Thank you kindly." Asar began to move the phone from his ear when Storm called his attention back.

"One thing I require..."

"What is it?" The agitation in Asar's voice was no longer masked.

"Please extend an invitation to her... she is to come to Dragon Loch directly... I very much need to speak with her."

"Her?" Asar was confused. Alex couldn't have known of Azrael.

"The demon," he replied dryly. "And it is not an optional invite."

"What? Alexander, are you mad? What makes you think she will comply with such a request?"

"Please old man, you are most persuasive when you wish to be... think of something. God speed."

"Alexander..."

There was no reply.

Sliding the phone back into his pocket, Asar joined the others, cursing and mumbling under his breath as he went.

"Everything all right, big guy?" Keith could see the distress in his eyes. It made him nervous. Very nervous.

Asar, catching sight of the boy's concern, quickly eased his mind. "Yes, yes... All is fine... Shall we?"

To that, Azrael stepped forward and placed her dainty, soil-stained hand in his and began to lead him further into the building. Her touch was surprisingly warm, and Asar was sure he felt a wave of earnest, peaceful calm wash over him. He peered down at the child through the corner of his eye. She wore a content smile upon her face. *How peculiar this little one is,* he thought to himself. She was adorned in tattered and weather-beaten rags, unwashed, and just a downright mess. Yet she carried herself with poise and confidence, leading them on into the unknown.

"Just around this bend," she said, tugging on his hand and breaking the spell.

Pausing, he pointed to an alcove that appeared to be fairly sturdy with a doorframe at its center. The pitted and peeling paint that covered the molding of the frame gave way to strong steel columns beneath. It would be safe for Azrael, even if the structure began to collapse.

"Why don't you wait here, my dear," Asar said. He pointed to the doorless frame, ushering her to where he wanted her to stand. "I am not so confident this building wishes to remain standing much longer."

She laughed. "Is it tired?"

"Ha. Yes, I believe it *is* rather tired, and we don't want it to go lying down right on top of you, do we?"

"You are just being silly now, Asar. I am not a baby."

"I never meant to..."

She cut him off sharply with her hand, putting one finger over her lips.

"I will come with you," Azrael whispered back playfully. "He will watch over me," she said, continuing to point at Keith. "You save William," she winked and began walking the last few steps to Decker. "That's the plan."

Asar shook his head at Keith, who shrugged in return.

"Be ready now," Asar said, tapping Keith on the shoulder. "Vigilance is key."

The two grown men followed the tiny girl into the darkness.

25

No lights. No gunfire. No one shouting his name intermingled with Egyptian curses. Frank Jericho had travelled far enough downstream to be free of his turncoat guide and whoever that other group was that had happened upon the two of them on the edge of the Nile. He hadn't travelled very far though - essentially allowing the current to carry him north. The mystical characteristics of the Nile included water that flowed northward to the Mediterranean Sea, escaping the land at the Nile Delta. This had been extremely advantageous for Jericho, as he had no wish to travel further inland in a southernly direction. Over there he would find only darkness and desert as one approached the outermost southern borders of Egypt. No, he would continue north and reach Luxor by morning, but first he needed to find a section of embankment that would allow him to withdraw from the water and still be afforded some degree of cover.

Spying what appeared to be a small cluster of boulders about twenty yards ahead, just on the outskirts of the water, he set course for the temporary shelter, pushing his legs hard against the force of the river as he walked.

"Two-minute break," he whispered to himself. The waterway

pulled a slight curve which created a minuscule, but formidable section of churning water. Jericho decided it would be best to exit now, before entering the disturbance in the Nile's flow. It could be rocks or even a gargantuan croc - something was acting as an impediment to the flow, and there was no way for him to see what it was.

Frank abruptly hoisted himself out of the water, making his way across the small greenery that was littering the shore on the river's edge. Scurrying quietly to the rock formation, he quickly appraised the surface area, which was visible in the light of the moon. Unsurprisingly, the cluster was comprised of several chunks of limestone, which covered most of the exposed surface of Egypt in great abundance.

Paying especially close attention to a jutting, bench-like ledge, he brushed away the sand and debris that had accumulated there over millennia, and feeling satisfied as to the spot's safety, took a seat to rest his bones a moment and regroup.

"Luxor... Luxor... Luxor," he whispered. Once again, he appeared to be addressing the moon. "Luxor, dead ahead." Jericho shifted in the hard rock and performed a double eyebrow raise as his words resonated in the canals of his ears.

"Not *dead* ahead," he said, shaking his head now and keeping himself company with humor. "Just *ahead*... let's skip the dead portion of that statement, shall we?" He chuckled faintly at his own superstitious idiosyncrasies.

Staring at the reflection of the moon as it danced and rippled across the surface of the flowing water, Jericho could feel his resolve begin to recharge in the therapeutic, nearly mesmeric din of sound and imagery. He was truly "naked in the rain" as the old saying went, and he would be forced to barter and most likely plead for assistance and charity from the good people of Egypt if he had any hopes of returning to his hotel room and hightailing it out of there. He would stay out of the water for now, traverse the river's edge as best he could, and keep on track until he made Luxor. Once there, he would hopefully be able to use a few name drops and get himself and Alexander's artifacts (which still lay in the lightweight water bag strewn loosely about his neck) back to Cairo.

The momentary peace of the night was instantly shattered by the whirl and churn of a helicopter closing in at breakneck speeds.

"What the fuck?!"

The words bellowed from deep in Jericho's chest. They were out here for *him*, no doubt about it. Choppers around these parts don't have a habit of taking to the air in the night. Too many unknowns. Sandstorms and rapidly-changing wind patterns helped reserve flights in this region to daytime, or, as was the case here, emergencies.

Who the hell is Aptera? Frank wondered, exchanging glances with the moon once again while pondering the influence of his simple native guide. *And how'd they locate me so fast?*

He was on his feet now and his plans gone to hell, Jericho headed towards the water once more. He had quickly surmised that being submerged was the way to go, as his predominately bare dark skin would stand out against the soft, white colors of the desert terrain. In the shadowy water of the Nile, he would blend together with his surroundings and be able to dive down, completely out of view for intervals.

"And yet another reason why it's great to be a beautiful black man," he muttered, laughing, and sucked in a powerful heaping of air before diving headlong back into the ancient waters. He had spied the outer edges of a massive spotlight in his peripheral vision just as his head entered the water, and he catapulted down with a massive breaststroke, tumbling around under the water so that he could peer upward at the surface. The chopper was overhead, and the brilliance of a mega-powerful search light trolled across the water above him. Steadying himself, Frank held out one arm and looked at it for traces of recognition as it descended through the water's surface.

Just barely, he thought to himself, as he spun downward and repeated the process once more to bring himself a little deeper into the river. This time his arm gave no indication that it was visible from the light above. He calmed himself and slowed his heart. He had always been able to do this. The first time he recalled achieving this

Zen-like feat, he was no more than ten years old. He, his cousin, and a bunch of other kids from the neighborhood were jerking around at the Miller & Sons Salvage Yard. It was an old-school-style junk yard in the heart of the Bronx that had gone out of business years earlier. Remnants of trash, cars, and appliances littered the dirt-floored yard and made the perfect terrain for everything from war with cap guns to good old-fashioned hide-and-seek.

That was the game they were engaged in on that hot and humid July morning. They all knew they weren't supposed to be in the yard. It was cyclone-fenced up, and "Keep Out" signs had been posted on virtually every inch of the fencing. The boys had found a flipped-up corner in the fence the previous fall and had since been using the apocalyptic field as their very own world. So, hide-and-seek it had been. What was it they used to call it? It was something much more macho and foreboding. "Hide-and-seek" was for girls and children. They were men. The game needed a name to fit.

"Oh yeah," he remembered as his left side spoke to his right in the gloom of the river at night. "Manhunt! That was it."

So, Manhunt it was. His cousin James, a few years younger than him, was riding on his coattails. Jericho recalled really giving it to him. James had been attached to him all summer, and it was time for him to man up, as it were.

"Find your own spot," he had demanded. "Stop following me."

Jericho clearly recalled the hurt in the young boy's eyes. How was it that he could recall the pain in someone's eyes from forty or fifty years ago, but he could not recall the imagery of his wife's eyes, full of love and appreciation, from just a short time ago. She was gone, and he really wished he could relive that common, daily vision in his mind's eye right now.

Anyway, once the boys split up, Jericho had headed to an old Frigidaire clunker towards the back of the yard. He had spied it days earlier but figured it was too tight for two people, so he had avoided it with James attached at the hip. Now was his chance. Once inside, he would ride out this session of Manhunt to victory. Accolades would come in aplenty, and he would surely be crowned the King of the

Hunt. He had peered over his shoulder once more to appraise the progress of his cousin, and found him moving through the rows of stacked bric-a-brac hesitantly. He had yelled then, yelled to James, yelled at him. He didn't recall his exact words, but they were borne of frustration, borne of youth and intended to shame his cousin.

The next incidences, he was able to recall without any issues - the dank, musty smell of the old refrigerator - the sound of the clasp engaging - and the air seal sucking as he pulled the door shut behind him. The fact that he recalled instantly thinking, "What have I done?" as the chamber went pitch black and outside sound ceased spoke to his carelessness, at best. That, he remembered all too well. It was here in this cube of terror and death that Frank Jericho first trained himself to control his respiration. His heart. His breath. He had no choice. He had canceled the terror - immediately. He was mentally sharp, even at that age, and he knew the air was limited, so yelling, banging, or panicking would all result in the same issue. Depleting his air very quickly would mean suffocation in minutes.

He had slowly thought of the positives of his situation, and in turn closed down his breathing and calmed his brain. There were only four of them that day, thank God! Usually, eight was their number, but Billy got the bug and passed it to half of them, so he had one Hunter and only himself, James, and Richie to find. James would most likely get caught instantly, then they would go for Richie, and then him. Ten minutes. He needed ten minutes. At least, that was what he told himself, and that was his last thought. After that, he did something he had never been trained to do - something that had just come instinctively - a survival trait hardwired in his genes.

His heart slowed to a crawl, to maybe twenty beats per minute. His air intake was so limited that he probably could have spread out that fridge's supply for two hours. He hadn't, however, needed to survive that long. James had been eyeing him - he hadn't been able to help it - and James had seen where Jericho had hidden. Frank figured about ten minutes had ticked by before hard bangs shocked him back to reality. Sharp thuds... followed by shards of light flowed over Frank, and he lurched from his tomb like a bullfrog. Using James as a cushion, the two boys hit the ground with a thud. Frank had squeezed his cousin so tight that afternoon.

"You saved me," Jericho had blurted out, "you saved me, James. I would have suffocated in there."

"Oh..." His cousin's eyes wandered as he took the whole thing in, recognition finally grasping him. "So I guess I'm a man now, too?" His chin had gone up proudly.

"You sure the hell are, James... you sure the hell are."

And once again, Jericho could recall the hurt and pain in the boy's eyes when he rejected him on that steamy inner-city afternoon. He could not, however, recall the pride and joy in James' eyes when he praised him for his rescue. Still, Jericho knew it had been there - and that would have to be sufficient.

Returning to the present, he realized the searchlight and the faint buzz of the rotors was gone. He exhaled sharply and pumped himself up and into the night air.

26

"Dr. Awain, at your service."

With a slight bow, the smartly dressed, middle aged man seized Jade's hand and touched it ever so softly to his lips. She eyed him attentively as his gaze worked its way surreptitiously over her body. He seemed rather skilled at this exercise, that being the visual undressing of the object of his attention without giving much indication that he was doing so. Jade had caught it though, and she would use it.

Through the years she had created a mental notebook of the various shades and models of men she encountered. Their idiosyncrasies, peculiarities and weaknesses were always useful to know. Jade was all too aware that any interaction she had with a man, especially in this part of the world, always began with her at a disadvantage. By being able to discern minute changes in facial expressions, the turn of an eye, a precisely placed laugh or other nervous tell, the position of the arms, or even what her subject was doing with his hands, she was able to approach those exchanges with a proverbial leg up. And hey, if that didn't work, she could always resort to the literal legs up. It was all part of the grand theatrics - the drama of life - orchestrated to escape the mundane, the self-loathing, and the disappointment with one's self that so many men in Awain's age group experienced. Add the education and the status, and it just ramped up the oddities that passed for civilized, adult behavior.

The same scenarios played out on the stage between Atticus and the audience. And oddly enough, she was fairly sure that the prejudices contemplated in the minds of the audience members were the same as those that reared themselves in her one-on-one interactions - including the one she was presently engaged in. Atticus was surely considered the "boss," and she, the female in the act, mere arm candy to distract the crowd and enable him to do his thing. Ultimately, her learned experience broke it down into two groups - men she could control with sex, and men she couldn't. Dr. Awain was wholeheartedly a member of the first. In fact, she surmised in a matter of seconds that he could actually be that group's leader.

Jade laughed on the inside and bat her eyes twice very slowly. The good doctor shifted on his heels, indicating to Jade that her subtle, yet erotic, eye movement had registered.

"Well," Awain said, beginning to catch sight of Atticus to her rear. "Oh, my apologies, sir."

"He didn't even see you there, dear Atticus," Jade remarked, as she turned and toyed with him.

"Do forgive me," the doctor said, genuine regret coming across in his voice. "And you are?"

"My assistant," Jade interjected, intercepting his path to Atticus. "He's here to assist." She smiled and touched Dr. Awain's shoulder.

"Oh," he replied and laughed nervously. "Lucky chap."

"Yes, well, that remains to be seen." She gave him a sly grin and touched his shoulder once again. She felt him tremble ever so slightly. This was going to be too easy.

"Well, you will have to forgive me, Miss... ahh?"

"Narra Mar," she replied.

"Yes, of course, Miss Mar. I am afraid someone may have been derelict in their duties. There appears to be an omission of a note to me, or a calendar entry for that matter. I have nothing on my calendar."

"And if I had to guess, it was probably a woman," Jade offered with a big jovial breath that clearly caught her host off-guard.

"Well, I..." he finally said, fighting to recover while wearing a grimaced look on his face.

"Oh, my..." Jade replied. "I just assumed by how well-dressed and groomed you were that you had prepared for this."

"Well..." He again trembled uncontrollably. "No, this is just me."

"Fascinating," she offered. "No stuffy, unkempt scientists here, I see."

"Which leads me to the point at hand. That being, that I am at a loss for both the purpose and the requirements of your visit."

Jade began to walk in the direction Awain had arrived from. "You were going to give us a brief tour of the museum and grant us some insight into what it takes to run such a highly respected institution."

"Splendid," he chimed in and began to follow her. She could sense his eyes trained on her ass. Stopping abruptly, she spun to face him again. "And, of course, you were going to give us an up-close look-see at it."

"It?"

"The scroll, silly," she stated matter-of-factly. "What did you think I meant?"

The guard had outpaced the three of them, already holding the door to the inner sanctum of the museum open.

"Yes, of course," he reassured Jade. "I am not sure how 'up-close' we can get, but I will allow several photographs if your assistant is so inclined."

Jade nodded as the trio made their way past the soldier and into the brightly lit hall of the museum's back offices.

"Lead the way, then," Jade requested.

"To the scroll?" Awain questioned, almost hurt. "I thought perhaps we could begin in my office and then make our rounds throughout the museum. Your assistant could get some photographs of me at my desk."

Jade heard the clasp and lock affix as the doorway they had just passed through sealed behind them, "Oh, silly man," she whispered.

"Excuse me?" he asked, rather unsure of what she had murmured.

Ignoring Dr. Awain, she continued to walk on and made her way past him so that he was now in between her and Atticus.

"The Copper Scroll," she demanded, her demeanor suddenly changing like a summer storm front. "Take us to the scroll now."

"I don't..."

"Understand?" she finished. "Atticus, help the good doctor understand."

With that, Atticus withdrew a rather ominous looking weapon from the recesses of his jacket. The compact, yet extremely deadly Skorpion submachine gun was capable of firing hundreds of rounds per minute. Atticus flipped down the folded stock and trained the weapon on the doctor.

"Understand now?" Jade purred.

"I don't want any trouble," he gasped, putting his hands above his head.

"That's too bad, Doc, because you found it." She laughed and motioned him on. "Or perhaps, I should correct that. Trouble has found *you*. The scroll. Now!" she demanded.

Dr. Awain said no more. He did not want to die in the back hall of a museum. Leading the duo around a sharp bend, he arrived at a large metallic plate in the wall. Atticus turned to Jade and shrugged. Moving the gun closer to him, Atticus made a gesture to proceed, but the doctor waved him off.

"The scroll," he quickly explained. "It's here. Behind the steel wall."

"Open it!" Jade had had enough. She felt him stalling. "Open the fucking wall. You have three seconds, or I'm going to open you and your pretty suit with my bare hands."

Sensing the newfound urgency, Dr. Awain ran his hand over the wall to the left of the steel plate and slid open a rather well-camouflaged control panel. Jade stepped forward and looked at the setup. There was a red button in the center and a key receptacle on either side of the button.

"I... I..." Awain stumbled over his words like a baby learning to walk. "I need the other key."

"Where is your key?" Jade demanded. She watched as he loosened his tie and unbuttoned the top of his well-tailored silk shirt. Reaching in, he withdrew a long chain with an ornate key on the end. Snatching the chain from him, she walked over and looked at the panel.

"Which side is yours?"

"The left," he rapidly responded.

"Who has the second key?" She was all business now, and her dark Asian eyes burned with fury.

"Sailor," he muttered. His dark nomadic skin was growing paler by the second. "Mr. Sailor, Head of Museum Security."

"Call him here," she hissed. "Now!"

Atticus leveled the machine gun at his head to speed the process along. Without looking up at him, the doctor retrieved his cell phone and using the push-to-talk feature, barked into the phone, "Sailor, we have an emergency." His voice was authoritative. "I need to access the scrolls... bring your key."

There was silence, and Jade ushered him to speak more.

"Do you read me, Sailor?"

"Did you warn him?" Atticus said, breaking the silence by speaking for the first time since the doctor joined them. He pressed the gun's barrel into his ribs.

"No, no... of course not," he promised. "The signal is touch and go in here sometimes..."

Atticus felt his finger take on a mind of its own, as involuntary pressure began play upon the Skorpion's trigger.

"Don't!" Jade demanded, staring directly at him. Shaking off his trance of anger and aggression, Atticus slid his finger off the trigger, resting it behind.

The curator's phone buzzed to life and a static-shrouded voice broke the momentary silence.

"Sailor here," the security officer finally replied. "What's going on, sir? Is everything all right?"

Dr. Awain looked back and forth at his captors who were shaking their heads in unison.

"You were just saved by the bell, Awain baby... let's not ruin it with your body being turned into Swiss cheese, okay?"

With that, the doctor spoke rapidly into the phone. "I need the damn key! I said I had an emergency, that should be sufficient. Now stop questioning me and get your ass over here!"

"Ten-four," came the reply, and the line went silent.

Jade, arching backwards, performed an overly erotic sequence of stretches. Her taut, deeply rich and tanned body became exposed in several locations as her clothing lifted and shifted. She watched Dr. Awain through the corner of one eye and was amused, but not shocked, to find him hungrily studying her every move. Even now - standing toe-to-toe with the reaper - he could not control his appetite for the flesh. Mindless monkeys, all of them.

"How far?" she said, stopping her thirty-second peep show experiment.

"What?"

"How far, doctor? How long will it take for your head of security to join us?"

"Well..." He thought a moment. There would be no point in lying, and it would probably up the chances for bloodshed. "I would say about two more minutes if he left right away."

Jade signaled to Atticus, who forced the doctor to his knees and took position directly behind hm. The doctor whimpered slightly at this new compromised position and both of his assailants shushed him to be quiet.

Sailor rounded the corner and walked into the scene Jade had staged for maximum effect. She gave him no warning as she marched up to him. "Your weapon, now," she demanded. The officer screamed ex-military, and Jade could see the machinations transpiring behind his eyes.

"There is no way out... comply and live," she coaxed.

Sailor handed his weapon over, a standard police and military 9mm, and took a step back from Jade.

"Excellent!" she shouted. "See how well this is going? Last thing now for me... give me the second key."

"I don't have it," Sailor said, letting slip a sly smirk for just a second, but long enough for Jade to see it.

"You find this amusing, sir?" Her anger was at its boiling point instantaneously, and Sailor didn't like the morphing effect he noticed in her pretty, dark eyes.

"What the fuck, Awain?" he asked. But the doctor was not at the proper vantage point to see what he was seeing.

"Gentleman," she announced, extending her arms to the heavens and taking a step back. "May I introduce Atticus the Great!"

"Now?" Atticus asked, grinning from ear to ear.

Jade slinked like a cat to the far side of the hall. "Yes, Atticus the Great and Powerful... Now!"

Sailor ran to Dr. Awain's side and helped him to his feet. "What the fuck is going on?" the head of security demanded.

"They want the Copper Scroll..." Awain said, frantically. "We must stop them!"

It was too late. Atticus had already retrieved the ring from the small leather pouch in his pocket and was sliding it on his finger. He tossed the Skorpion to one side and gave his full attention to the task at hand. Chanting in an ancient dialect, he called forth fire and fury. Bellows of smoke rushed the hallway and all the exits. Spreading like a fog front on a morning pond, the low-lying mist covered every inch of the museum's floors.

Jade looked surprised. This incantation must be new, as she had never seen anything quite like it during any of the previous sessions. Sailor and Dr. Awain were clearly terrified, as they should be.

Then, with a blazing bright snap of blinding lightning, it was there. Asmodeus, the demon of legend, was there to do Jade's bidding.

The demon, who was by now well-versed with the evil sorceress that was Jade, stood ready to receive commands. She smiled at the apparition who had come to them from Hell in a much different form than before. A rotting and decaying hooded robe wrapped over its skeletal-like features. Besides the glowing eyes sunk deep within the hood, there were no other facial characteristics.

"Reap their souls," she demanded of the demon, stepping forward. "Then rip through that wall, mind the treasure on the other side, and retrieve the Copper Scroll!"

The demon's hood bowed almost indiscernibly, and it set to work.

"The key was... the key," Jade said, laughing over the doomed men's cries for mercy. "And now you will have an eternity in Hell to ponder your decision to be coy with me."

Positioning herself beside Atticus to get a better view of the carnage, she pridefully added, "And when you get to Hell, be sure to tell them Naamah says hello, and I miss them all, terribly!"

27

"Good God, man!" Asar shouted in sheer terror as he entered the abandoned dining hall of the resort. The room was strewn with the remnants of destroyed dining stations, and it appeared that every table and chair in the dank, lit room had been taken down at the legs. Debris and garbage littered the dirt-laden floors along with rotting leaves and other organic matter that had blown in through the openings to the outside balconies, which once contained glass panes for windows and grand size entry doors. The glass from those portions of the structure lay shattered in odd little piles, reminiscent of a child's sand play at the beach. The fine shards of glass sparkled and gleamed with the assistance of what little light entered into the room. Asar's eyes drifted about, taking stock of all of this, and he noted how the glass piles sublimated the light to create a galaxy of stars on the high ceilings above them.

The little girl had not paused along with her elders. She moved nonchalantly through the space, dodging and weaving debris in an obstacle course fashion until she arrived beside William Decker.

"I found your friends, William," she said, smiling at the slumped-over shell of a human. "And they have brought what you need." She moved in close and raised a cupped hand to her mouth. "They have the necklace, William."

At the center of the hall lay a slightly raised circular area. Asar surmised it was once a grand dance floor, encircled by a band of intense lights within the border that shone up and out, spotlighting happy resort guests as they boogied the night away. Now it was cracked, and no light would ever emanate from its surface again. He took a slight step forward through the rubble towards Decker and Azrael. His eyes had begun to adjust to the room's lighting, which was in shadow on one side and filled with sheer, bright sunlight on the other. He noticed how the light did not make it past the center of the room's dance circle, as if it were swallowed by some invisible mouth. It was there, at the shadow's edge, that a figure now came into view - a lanky, robed, and hooded apparition that hovered several feet off the decayed wood of the dance floor.

"Demon!" Asar called out as he allowed his legs to commence their trek to Decker. "Show yourself, Demon."

Low, gurgling laughter promptly replied to his words and filled the hall with echoing intensity. Keith grimaced and quickly caught up to Asar's side.

"Some insight now, please," he prodded, and was ignored.

The cacophony of mixed voices and laughter ceased as quickly as it had begun, and the cloaked demon drifted closer to the light's edge but did not cross.

"I am right here, old man." Her voice was feminine and familiar for some reason. Alexander had provided certain details regarding the mission. He had purposely reserved some key data, including the name of the demon holding Decker for ransom. That was what was happening, after all - a ransom exchange of metaphysical proportions was about to take place. Asar was all too well aware that due to Alexander's relationship with William, he may be engaging in very poor decision making right now. Needless to say, equipping any demonic entity with more firepower was of no assistance to their various plights, but if Asar was correct in his analysis of this witch's voice, this really was a bad idea.

"Dare I say... Bathin?"

The laughter sprang forth again.

"You sound surprised, pilgrim. Did your better not tell you whom you were coming to call on?"

"He did not," Asar said, puffing his chest. "As I am sure he knew I would have surely devised a method of banishing you, over bartering with the likes of your wretched being."

There was a long pause.

"Asar..." Decker's voice was strained and dry like the desolate winds blowing across the landscape outside. "Please... give it what it wants... I need to leave."

He looked at William now, propped in a crumbling wooden chair. His arms were dangling behind his back - locked in some form of demonic handcuffs. Glowing bands of ethereal matter clasped his wrists tightly together. His legs hung freely over the chair, which at one point must have been a bar stool or the like. It was shorter now, yet only the tips of his shoeless toes brushed the floor. Around him was a scattering of broken plastic bottles, old tin cans, and plastic bags. Asar looked up from the menagerie of trash and spied Azrael observing him contently.

"Water," she offered. "She let me bring him water," she repeated, signaling towards the objects on the floor.

"That was most heroic of you, young lady," Asar said, forcing a smile. "You have most likely saved William's life."

Smiling back, she reached out and rubbed Decker's shoulder. He lifted his weary head and returned the nicety.

"Young lady!" Bathin bellowed and laughed. "Ha!"

"Tend to them," Asar instructed Keith, who was crouching and investigating the spiritual bindings holding their victim in place. He nodded and rose upright.

Asar took several steps forward into the circle and reached into his inner vest pocket. Retrieving the bag that held the sacred jewels, he lifted it above his head.

"Demon!" he called, and before he could utter his next words, Bathin was across the circle and on him like a viper. She hovered at an immeasurable closeness, and the show of paranormal acrobatics took Asar's wind away.

"Yes..." Her breath stank of rot and all things unholy. "Give it here, pilgrim."

"Terms," Asar said, catching his breath. "There are terms."

"Listen to me you fat cocksucker! Here are the terms... give it to me, and I won't tear you all to pieces. First, I will pull the limbs from that wretched little dirt whore, and use them to bash each of your skulls in, in turn... how's *that* for terms, you miserable cunt?"

Asar surmised that this demon and her powers were limited. If not, she would have taken what she wanted already - but she had not. She was showing her cards and allowing her anger to defy her. Alexander had known this. This is why he was so sure she would abide by the request and let them all leave safely.

"Really?"

"Really," she growled.

"Do it."

"What? What did you say, filth?"

"Do it. Kill the girl. Beat us with her legs, or whatever other rubbish you were spewing. Did I get that right?"

Bathin's body and stature swelled with immense fits of anger. Had he been mistaken? Was she just playing nice and not truly constrained by anything? He was about to find out.

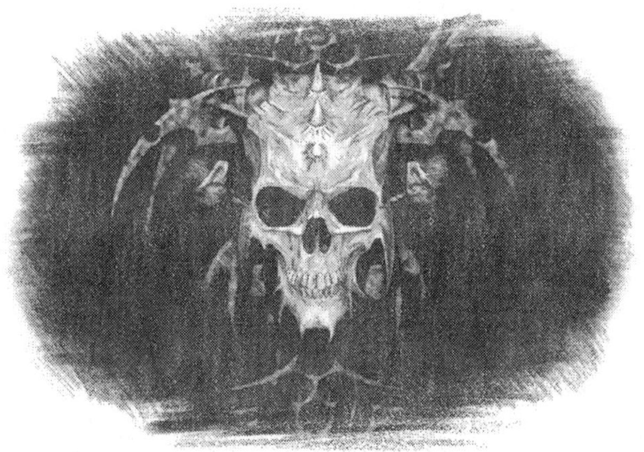

"Yes, do it!" he yelled.

"You got me," the demon hissed, sinking back, "Can't fault a girl for trying, right?"

"Asar," William implored once more, and Asar got the inclination that he may be in worse shape than he appeared to be on the surface.

"Terms..." Asar continued, returned his attentions to Bathin without answering William. "First and foremost, the four of us leave this wretched place, of our own accord, to where we wish to go ourselves - without any interference or assistance or intervention by you."

Asar knew he was currently playing the role of a demonic attorney, and he needed to cover all his bases on the terms of the exchange and release.

"Second, I shall place the necklace just out of your reach in the sunlight, as it appears you cannot venture into its rays. It will be approximately one hour away. Once the sun goes down enough, you will be able to retrieve the necklace. This ensures we have enough time to depart the area."

"The fat Egyptian's terms are accepted," she hissed.

The room's light was shifting, and Asar could finally see the beast at the back of the hood. Ancient and rotted, only a thin layer of crumbling flesh covered Bathin's bones. Her eyes were eerie pupils of pinpoint fire set amidst fathomless black sockets. A shiver ripped through his spine, but he held fast and did not betray his calm and collected exterior. He did not avert his eyes.

"There is one more caveat. If you please will allow me to finish, we may all be on our way."

"Asar..." Decker was clearly becoming more agitated. *Good,* Asar thought, *it will energize him for the move.* He looked back and forth between Azrael and Keith, who nodded in unison. They had him... he was okay.

"Third," he said, his voice powerful and unwavering. "Your presence is required at Dragon Loch Castle... immediately... upon..."

The demon's head flew back, and laughter and chortling sounds began to emanate from below the hood.

"Are you cracked?" Bathin rattled out. "Dragon Castle... Hahahaha!"

"Bathin! This is not negotiable. You are to port yourself to the Tea Room at Dragon Loch Castle immediately upon your departure from this room. No stops... no detours. I am told Mr. Storm requires five minutes of your time, and then you can be on your way to murder and pillage."

The demon stopped its theatrical display and turned back to Asar. "And rape," it echoed in multiple voices. "Let us not forget rape along with murder and pillage, or else what fun would any of it be? This I ask you wholeheartedly, fat Egyptian... what fun would it be?"

"Are the terms acceptable, serpent?" Asar demanded an immediate answer.

"Well, I can't say I wouldn't mind spending time with that delicious piece of meat, but what's to stop Storm from trapping me, reclaiming the necklace, and locking me away for eternity in some forgotten hole?"

"The word of Alexander Storm, that is what! And *that* is worth more than one single promise from all the occupants of Hell."

"Fair," she jested, turning to the others. "This is a fair characterization of the honor of our little community down yonder... so I won't take offense to the turning of a phrase."

"Do we have a deal?" Asar again demanded.

Rising high into the air, she spoke. "You have your deal... with the devil... I accept the terms."

Lifting one robed arm, Bathin allowed the vestiges of a few bony fingers to escape her loosely hanging garb, and pointing in Decker's direction, snapped her fingers. Decker groaned and fell sideways toward Azrael, freed from the mystical shackles. Keith reached out grabbed William's shoulders, stopping his body from clobbering the girl before falling to the floor. They scrambled to right the situation all under the watchful eye of Asar. Propping Decker over Keith's shoulder, the girl secured him at his hips, and the three rose to their feet to move.

Asar, sensing the move was upon them, stepped back into the bright light just beyond the interior of the dance floor circle. Placing the bag with the necklace down in the light, he rose quickly and, as fast as his large frame would carry him, relieved Azrael of her position.

"You will leave with us," he whispered to the girl. "There is nothing here for you."

Azrael squinted and grimaced at the men, contemplation spreading across her brow.

"That, my dear girl, is an order - there is nothing to consider."

She smiled and nodded. "All right."

"Guide us out now, if you will."

As the trio backed out of the hall, they watched as Bathin floated to the edge of the darkness, her hood trained on the small bag and its contents that lay just inches from her grasp. Asar felt a foreboding shockwave creep through his body as the demon began to engage in a very dramatic and accentuated string of movements, looking from the bag, to them, to her feet. Over and over she continued this farce, and Asar was horror-struck as she gingerly moved out of the darkness and into the light. Keith, watching this unfold, began to scream in objection. Asar silenced him with a glance.

"That," Decker said, straining under the pain of movement, "is what I tried tell you..." His words were broken and soft. "She can walk in the light just fine."

The four escapees froze as Bathin removed her hood, exposing the atrocity of her being to the light of day. Then, seizing the material of her robe at her chest, she yanked it free, ripping the dilapidated garment from her frame and exposing her rotting, dead, demonic frame to the captive audience. Smiling the rotted, toothy grin of the reaper, she bent and retrieved her prize from the floor.

The ornate stones of the necklace danced in the powerful rays of the descending Tunisian sun. Everywhere their brilliant light touched on the demon became instantly young and beautified. Holding the perfection of craftmanship high up to the light, Bathin sent strong gem reflections about the room in a parade of color and light. The group watched in horror as the necklace's rays had the exact opposite effects on their own bodies, turning their healthy living tissue into dead and rotted globs of flesh as the light passed over. All of them, that is, except the young girl, whose form the gem's brilliance had no effect on. Asar brushed it off to her youth, or perhaps her innocence and lack of sin, and so the concern regarding this anomaly within an anomaly left his thoughts.

Laughing a hideous, hyena-like laugh, Bathing unclasped the lock and wrapped the jewels around her throat. The first to morph was her laugh, which transgressed into a sweet and sultry expression. Her voice came next, the spoken word...

"Sinners, say your prayers... Judgment Day is here!"

She laughed again as her entire being rippled and floated like a vision of heat on summer pavement, and then... she was anew. Long flowing locks of red hair danced about her face and shoulders. Her skin became soft and supple. Her breasts became large, firm, and perfectly formed, as was her figure, which drifted like flowing water into her legs, which appeared to go on forever.

"Oh my God..." gasped Keith. The young man was immediately taken, Asar noted, as he loosened his grasp on Decker.

"She's a demon, my boy," Asar whispered loudly. "Evil incarnate... snap to... snap out now!" he demanded.

But it was falling on deaf ears, and Asar became more agitated. He was about to have a problem.

"I have been in that unsightly form for so long... Who wants to be my first? It's sure to be an energetic, unforgettable journey. How about you, pilgrim?" She pointed at Keith, sensing his weakness, and beckoned him over to her with her fingers. "Come on, come to me, and we will both cum over and over."

Asar heard the slight voice of Azrael as she tugged at Keith's shirt and stood upon her tippy toes to speak in his ear.

"Keith," Azrael went on, "she is the great deceiver... the temptress... the scarlet whore of Babylon... pray and break away..." Keith shifted, obviously struggling with the internal battle of the siren's call.

"Please Keith," Azrael spoke louder and with an odd tone. "Think of Kate... break free."

Asar's head spun to Azrael. He peered at her through the squinted eyes of a cognitive microscope. He had heard right, hadn't he? Kate. His focus broke as Keith came to and began an urgent move to the exit, yanking the trio in tow.

Looking back once more, Bathin was smiling and shaking her head.

"Oh well," she said after them. "What a boring, tired bunch. Thanks for the company, William. It was enlightening, to say the least. See you soon." She turned, and with the flick of her wrist, opened a portal to Dragon Loch.

"I think I shall pay a visit to Alexander just like this. Perhaps Storm will be *up* for a party? What say you?" She called to them once more, but the desolate room was empty, save for her naked body, and in the blink of an eye, Bathin was gone as well.

28

Frank Jericho's mother had not raised a thief. That much was sure and true. She had been the salt of the earth. Church every Sunday, and most Fridays and Saturdays too if she could swing it. With four brothers and sisters and six cousins who, although they had their own homes nearby, had unilaterally decided to call Auntie Ernesta's place home, his mom had her hands full. Everyone was always up with the sunrise, even on Sunday. When asked why, oh why couldn't they sleep in on the last day of the week, his mother would quip and reply that they didn't call it Sunday for no reason. We were supposed to greet the sun, the new day, every day, and cherish the life we had been blessed with, as well as food on the table, a roof over the table, and a big enough table for us all to be together every day... even Sunday.

School was important, but education was even more important, and as his mother always stated, there was a huge difference between the two. Beds needed to be made, and rooms and bathrooms had to be cleaned up, every day, before breakfast. In this way, mom, or Auntie Ernesta, taught the important ethics of work and entrepreneurial endeavors as she encouraged her small city of kids to offer to perform services for each other, whether making beds for a week for a dollar or being on trash duty and taking a quarter from everyone else. This taught so many lessons not learned in school, and was part of the good old education branch she spoke about. They were skills they needed to acquire to survive in this world. Mom did all this in a not-so-nice area of the Bronx, New York, and it paid off in the end. Doctors, lawyers and Indian chiefs made up the ranks of her children and her extended assemblage.

And the most amazing part, if that wasn't enough of a miracle for you, was that she did all this on her own. He had a dad he did not know, save for the pictures that were everywhere in the house, some home movies, and the tales of his mother and his aunts and uncles. His dad, Charles Jericho, was a lieutenant and chopper commander during the Vietnam War. The VC had taken him out just a day before the end of his fifth and final tour. They blew his damn chopper out of the sky as he rounded about a mountain peak to pick up a pinned-down company of infantry soldiers. He was a hero, of this Frank knew, but it didn't matter - he didn't have a dad, and he found out later that he had been ordered to stand down. There was good intel that that the enemy had big, heavily hidden mobile artillery in the area, and they didn't want him flying his big green bullseye over the bamboo treetops. He apparently surmised it was now or never – that he needed to get the small ground battalion out now, or risk losing them forever. The rest was history... done and over. The intel was good for once.

Anyway, getting back to the situation at hand, Luxor, Egypt was a long, long way from mom. Frank was freezing, bleeding, and in need of food, drink, and some shut eye. And although Momma Ernesta did not raise a thief, Jericho stole the long, linen thawb hanging on the laundry line outside the small run of tenements just about a mile from his ultimate destination. He was cold and would make up for the indiscretion, but tonight, he was the thief of Persia. He also needed to cover more than his body - he needed his face hidden from view as well.

Slipping the long robe over his aching, cold bones instantly sent a shockwave of hope through him. Bringing the hood up and over his head allowed it to sit far back, disappearing from view, and it took that hope and turned it into invincibility.

Stepping from the shadows, he reacclimatized to his surroundings and was about to set off down the second back road on his left, when he spotted a small boy squatting, rocking to-and-fro, and watching him closely. He had no doubt witnessed the crime of the thief Frank Jericho and was now holding this stranger's fate in his hands. Deciding once again that he was now invincible, Frank reached up, hugged himself, and shivered and shook as if cold. The boy nodded, and Jericho then held a finger to his lips and joined his hands together as if praying. The boy smiled, and his brilliant double row of bright whites shined at Jericho, letting him know he understood and was remaining as quiet as a mouse.

Now Frank approached the lad slowly, hood drawn, so they could see each other. Sitting cross legged in front of the boy now, he once again attempted to proceed with signs. Grabbing the pockets of the robe, he turned them inside out to allow the dust to sprinkle out and get taken by the breeze. The small Egyptian boy's smile faded, but he soon shrugged and shook his head. It was okay he had nothing to offer in return for his silence. Jericho reached out and tapped the boy fondly on the shoulder, mouthing "thank you."

Both of them rose to their feet. Then it dawned on Jericho. *My blade.* He was almost to his destination, and the boy could really make use of his knife and all the gadgets in the handle compartment. Holding a finger up as if to say hold on, he reached to his ankle and removed the hunting knife non-threateningly from its sheath. Spinning the blade in his palm, he held it out and offered it to the boy. "Take," he mouthed. "For you."

The Egyptian boy slowly reached out, but instead of taking the blade, he reached down and grabbed Frank's other hand, bringing them both together on the knife. Then in a symbolic motion, the boy pushed Jericho's hands with the knife, to his chest.

"Keep," the boy whispered. "Need," he finished.

Frank Jericho, humbled by both the gesture and the entire interaction as a matter of fact, bowed gently to the boy and donned his hood.

"Thank you," he managed in an almost unintelligible tone. "Be safe."

Frank smiled to himself as he turned to leave.

I guess he has a Momma Ernesta at home too, he thought, smiling to himself.

"Francis," said a voice from behind him, which froze him, dead in his tracks.

"Francis," said the voice again, and he pivoted, but there was no one save the boy, whose back was now to him, about to round the corner into the last darkness of the night.

"Francis... avoid the Princess - they are waiting for you."

There was no doubt about it. The small Egyptian boy, who had kept Frank's thieving silent, was speaking to him clear as day, in a voice that seemed hauntingly familiar.

"Morris Hotel instead. The Dragon Storm awaits your arrival."

Overcoming his shock, Frank started after the boy, but as he had expected, the boy was gone.

He had no time to give chase. Turning to face the Nile at the end of the neighboring rows of buildings ahead of him, he noticed that a faint glow of orange was spreading across the horizon. He had very little time left, and he could already hear the commotion of families rising in the homes around him.

Taking one more moment to isolate his fastest route to the Morris, he took off. He intended to follow the boy's advice to a tee - no doubt about that.

"Fucking Alexander Storm," he whispered to himself as he ran, a smile creeping across his tired, beat-up face.

"Fucking Storm."

29

"The transport is arriving, Alexander," Philip announced as he shuffled by on his way to the loading docks of Dragon Loch Castle.

"Very good." Storm's reply was seeped in other thoughts, and he did not look up at the castle caretaker.

"Shall you be meeting with them first off?" Philip had paused and was peering with concern at the uncharacteristically disheveled appearance of his employer.

Alexander said nothing. Philip took a few steps back in his direction, his footsteps echoing in the stone-encased antechamber of the castle.

"Alexander, are you all right?"

"Quite all right," he replied, still studying the time-stained documents in his hands.

"Quite all right?" Philip repeated back at him.

"Yes, quite all right!" Alexander dropped his arms to his side in frustration. "Damn it, man what is it? I am trying to read this... I will speak to the girls in short order... there is nothing wrong with me, save the commonplace issues that plague my existence." He paused, noting the subtle indications of shock on his old friend's face. "I have eaten my breakfast, taken my vitamins and," he said, pausing for effect, "brushed my teeth."

Philip's expression morphed to one of annoyance, and he turned to depart. "Someone is a tad of a prick this fine morning, isn't he?"

"Philip!" Storm let a whole-hearted laugh escape the confines of his tense being. "Lead the way, old man."

The pair arrived just in time to see Anika and Abigail disembark, their luggage and other belongings trailing behind them as the crew of the Tiamat escorted the women to Alexander.

"Ladies!" Storm opened his arms with a warm embrace. "I trust your quick voyage was pleasant?"

"If you like boats," Anika said, laughing nervously.

"Well, your affinity for boats should have no bearing on this voyage, as you travelled here on a ship."

Philip rolled his eyes. "Here we go again... the whole *ship* nonsense." Taking Anika's hand, he instructed "Ignore him. Come, I have prepared you both a lunch of light fare with the other ladies."

Anika stopped and tapped Philip's hand affectionately. Her intent to have him relinquish his hold and do away with the niceties was immediately apparent.

"No offense," she said, nodding ever so briefly at Philip before turning to Alexander. "But I want to speak with you... about William... now."

Storm nodded and lifted a hand, settling her before she said more. "William Decker is safe and in the company of Asar and Keith."

"But..."

"They are in the process of securing passage to Italy, I believe, and from there, to Dragon Loch."

"I have not been able to get in touch with him for over a week." Anika's words acted as a dismissive catalyst that threatened to open the flood gates of her undoubted days of worry and imaginative contemplation of William's situation.

"Miss Anika," Alexander spoke strongly. "I promise you, I have been aware of William's location, his company, and his actions. I dispatched Asar to gather him up, at both great peril and ultimately, great cost, but Asar has been successful with the assistance of Keith, and William will be returning to you as we speak."

"Where was he?" Anika stepped out from between the two men and stood beside Abi. "What was he doing? Was it something for you, Storm?"

"Once again, I assure you all is well."

Alex turned from her and took a few steps towards the interior of the castle. The incoming tide sloshed and churned the salty water of the Atlantic against the ancient stone that lined the walls of the boat slip. When arriving at Dragon Loch Island, a boat must pass several security measures at the head of the island's land mass, then travel up a channel towards the castle. The channel dips as it reaches the massive structure and runs down into the castle interior. If one were watching the nautical maneuvers from the air, a ship would appear to disappear into the castle walls. The interior slip allowed for ships and boats of all sizes to dock and gain entry into the castle through a set of winding staircases terminating on the main floor. A massive freight elevator, one of Alexander's modern architectural additions, had been added several years earlier and was ideal for lifting deliveries and luggage to the main floors. Although guests were free to ascend via the newer mechanical means, most chose to use the stone staircases whose walls were lined with a series of small windows, which gave way to beautiful views of the castle, the island, and the horizon of the Atlantic Ocean. Clearly this vast body of water was no slouch when it came to picturesque views of the sun's coming and going.

Sensing that no one had moved, Alex spun on his heels and addressed Abigail.

"My dear Abigail, my apologies... We have been caught up in the drama of William Decker, once again," he remarked with equal measures of pensive annoyance and lighthearted ribbing. Anika did not smile. "You appear rested and refreshed. I am sure you are looking forward to seeing Kate and Samantha..."

"Samantha?" She jumped forward, past Anika. "Sam is here?"

"Yes, yes..." Alex was delighted to energize a new topic. "She is upstairs with Kate and Serket... Shall we?"

Arriving at the dining hall, Philip made a grand gesture of opening the door and called out, in royal announcement fashion, "Miss Abigail and Miss Anika!"

The three women who had been seated around the table rose to greet their newly arrived cohorts. Hugs and excited greetings ensued as Alexander kept vigil just beyond the circle of human interaction. He watched, listened, and soaked in the level of familiarity and companionship the group had developed in what was truly a short period of time.

"Holy crap, Abi," Sam went on, walking around her and looking her up and down. "What the hell happened to you? You fall into a vat of couture? You are fucking stunning!"

Abigail laughed. "Mr. Storm said I looked rested and refreshed. I believe those were his words." The women all turned in unison and shook their heads at their socially naïve host.

"Rested?" Kate interjected. "She looks like a different person."

Alexander smiled and said nothing. He had recognized that there were some changes to her dress, her makeup and hair, but it was something new he saw that made him really take notice. Confidence. And in Abigail's case, that was a very necessary and important trait to have in abundance.

In the clear light of the room, Storm took a moment to examine her appearance more closely. Her face and makeup were impeccable, with the application bringing out her strong, attractive features and accentuating her dark eyes. Abigail's hair had been straightened and was long and flowing. He found the soft, shiny curls cascading down and across her face in a professionally stylized manner to be quite alluring. Although Alexander was well-versed in the garb and attire of ancient societies, he was not so similarly situated in the current trends and styles of modern fashion. He did, however, have a keen eye for beauty and symmetrical design. That being said, even his lack of insight into contemporary fashion could not detract from his recognition that Abigail was wearing expensive, modern designs.

Alexander arrived at the conclusion that the others were, in fact, correct. The trifecta of her physical appearance, clothing, and most importantly, self-confidence, had, in essence, resulted in the presentment of a "new person." Alexander simply surmised that she looked lovely and required no further insight. Perhaps he had been lacking in his reaction upon her disembarking and decided to rectify it now.

"They are all correct, Abigail. Please forgive me for not noticing you." He said, clearing his throat. His words resulted in even more stares. Serket was shaking her head.

"Not to say I didn't notice you." He very quickly realized he should have stayed quiet on the subject. "What I mean is, I am sorry I didn't notice your changes, which are quite evident, and I am walking myself up against a wall here," Alex uttered, smiling nervously.

"Mr. Storm," Abigail began, but was quickly silenced by a motion from Alexander.

"Abigail, you look very lovely," he said, and smiled sincerely. Hoping to cut the conversation short, he signaled for them all to have a seat.

"Serket, I ask that you and the others bring Abigail and Anika up to speed. I also need for all of you, especially you Kate, to really pour over the news. We are looking for any and all anomalies - anything strange or out of the ordinary. Due to the "spin" of the modern cast of cable news coalitions, you may have to delve a bit deeper. Follow your gut on this one. If something doesn't feel right... investigate it further."

Alexander rose from the table, sliding his chair back pensively. "Feel free to catch up and all that, but this *is* a requisite task. I am fully confident we... I... am missing something. Have a pleasant evening. Philip will attend to your needs."

With several quick steps, Alexander was at the door. He paused as the women called after him in unison, questioning his departure.

"I have several side projects to deal with and, ah..." he said, gazing at his watch. "Oh yes, and if Asar was sufficiently persuasive, a date with a demon."

30

The Jordanian Museum echoed with panic and alarm as sirens bellowed out emergency warnings. Word of the antics of Naamah's demonically driven burglary was, undoubtedly, spreading like wildfire. She could hear traces of harried voices from beyond the walls. Screams in Arabic rang out like shrill thunder against the backdrop of incoming police and emergency services sirens. The Jordanian police had recently installed vehicle sirens much like those used by the European police forces, and their eerie, apocalyptic cadence provided a surreal soundtrack for the night's endeavors.

"What now?" pondered Atticus, who was hunched over and peering through the hole the demon had ripped in the wall to retrieve the Copper Scroll. He could make out the legs of uniforms scurrying to-and-fro, their wearers clueless as to what was transpiring just beyond their view.

Naamah did not answer. Instead, she remained on all fours studying the ancient scroll. The demon had retrieved the entire tray from the display and placed the three compartmentalized boxes on the floor at her feet.

Receiving no response from his partner-in-crime, Atticus moved, positioning himself behind her prone body. Studying her morphed appearance intently, he finally made his presence known.

"What's with the new look, baby?"

Silence.

"Hey!" he yelled, leaning over and slapping her tight bottom with his open palm. "I'm talking to you."

Naamah responded with furious speed, spinning and driving her shoulders into him with supernatural force, sending him toppling over backwards. Caught off guard, Atticus rose onto his elbows and stared across the floor at the crawling demon. With slow, precise movements, she was on top of him, staring down into his bloodshot eyes.

"Careful, Atticus the Great," she announced. "There are boundaries, my dear."

He struggled to scramble away from the eyes of the stranger who was speaking to him. Her entire appearance had changed. No longer of Asian descent, her features had become more akin to a European lineage, with dark, olive skin, shadowy, almost black eyes, and long, flowing brunette hair. She still had one overwhelming feature in common with her past self, though - she was absolutely, breathtakingly gorgeous.

Naamah, sensing his fear and lack of understanding, was already granting him a pass for his juvenile transgressions.

"Relax, handsome," she finally purred at him. "It's me... the *real* me."

A cloud of incomprehension remained over Atticus. She would need to deal with this now - she needed him here, in the present. Rising to her feet, Naamah extended a hand and yanked Atticus up. They stood nose-to-nose.

"This is my true self," she quickly explained, taking note of the increasing march of the militia gathering in the center of the museum. "Jade was simply a useful disguise to afford me the element of surprise against my enemies. They all believed I had been destroyed, and it made it much easier for me to operate as Jade. But the time has come for my return - for the return of *Naamah*."

"Naamah?" Atticus repeated, a hint of recognition in the notes of his voice. "Naamah... You are Naamah?"

"Indeed," she said, laughing. "You, my friend, have been fucking a demon."

Atticus, allowing his defenses to finally subside, smiled at the thought. It made him happy. It made him feel powerful.

"Fucking a demon," he repeated to himself.

"Listen," Naamah said, "We need to deal with this situation, or it's going to get out of hand rather quick. Not that I mind the carnage, of course."

"Of course..."

"I would just prefer to keep a low profile, for the time being."

This was a low profile? Fuck. Atticus nodded. He understood. As long as she was still *with* him, and not *against* him, they could sort this out later. Besides, this new Jade was really fucking hot, so there was that.

"I'm going to dispatch Asmodeus to deal with the military and the police. You and I need to work on the scroll so we can make our escape."

Atticus turned from Naamah and nodded his head in agreement as he walked, then retrieved his firearm from the floor. Checking the magazine and the action, he readied himself.

The archaic demon Asmodeus remained motionless, awaiting its master's commands.

"Destroy them all!" Naamah ordered, and the hooded demon snapped to, bowing its head in acknowledgment, and was gone.

"Grab the trays and bring them to the security desk around this corner," she instructed her companion. When it was found in Qumran Cave 3 in 1952, the brittle metal was still rolled in the classic form of a scroll. It had taken years of learned thought to devise a method to unravel and cut the scroll into flat strips that could easily be read.

Setting the trays containing the Copper Scroll down, the two began to study it closely. The Copper Scroll, as it had come to be known, was actually one of the famed Dead Sea Scrolls discovered in Qumran. What set the document apart was two very peculiar characteristics. The first oddity was that it had been drafted on sheets of copper rather than reed papyrus or linen. It was the only scroll from the region prepared in this manner, and the drafter had undoubtedly used this material to ensure the long life of the document. The second anomaly was, in fact, the document itself - for the Copper Scroll spun no tales of armies, wars, or prophecy. It was not a grouping of mantras, prayers, or religious texts. No, it was something much more tangible - something much more attainable. The Copper Scroll was simply stated, a treasure inventory and directional map. A treasure map! Outlined in the Scroll's text were the locations of sixty-four hordes of treasure - gold, silver and the like, secreted away millennia ago. The treasure was spread out across the land in a haphazard maze of riddles and directions with no starting points or orientations. Naamah surmised that this was most likely done due to the sudden invasion by a foreign army or a growing order of religious zealots.

"In the ruin that is in the Valley of Achor..." Naamah's voice trailed off as she travelled line-by-line with her finger through the text. "A distance of forty cubits... a strongbox filled with silver."

"Not only a sex machine," Atticus exclaimed watching her intently, "but a super nerd as well."

"Excuse me?" Naamah said, peering up from the scroll.

"You can actually read this, Jade," he said, then cleared his throat. "Er... Naamah. It's just lines and shapes to me."

"Well, yes," she said, smiling. "You are clearly not a nerd. However," she added, "you're a decent lay, so I shall keep you around a bit longer."

Atticus laughed nervously. He found himself conflicted between the compliment and what was ultimately a threat. His contemplation of exactly how long "a bit longer" hopefully was, was shattered by a burst of gunfire and screams. Debris dropped from the ceiling as a shower of tiles rained down from above, depositing white fibrous patches all over the desk. Naamah spun her long cape-like jacket in a dervish-like manner and shielded the Copper Scroll from the onslaught of asbestos flurries.

There had been a tremendous blast in the outer building, and everyone seemed to be converging on the hooded creature who, for the time being, was unstoppable.

"We need to hurry," Naamah said, drawing Atticus' attention back to the artifact. "We haven't much time."

Naamah returned to her study, instructing Atticus to stand watch. She did not want to be caught off guard, nor did she want any explosives or a firefight to break out in the back hall and threaten the safety of the scroll.

"I've got it," she spoke softly. "Column eight."

Atticus watched in admiration as she mouthed the ancient symbols, translating them in her mind. *Do demons have minds? Brains?* he wondered. His thoughts were wiped clean as Naamah began to giggle, almost like a small girl.

"What is it?" He said, half-heartedly laughing as he asked the question.

"All these years," she said, looking up at him. "All these the fools had it all wrong."

Atticus abandoned his post near the tear in the wall and moved to her side. "How's that?"

"It's all about the nuances, Atticus. These 'nerds,' as you so aptly coined them, were mesmerized by the fantastic list of treasures, gold, silver, and the like. The presence of a book in the middle of this obfuscating nightmare is only mentioned in passing. In fact, I've even noticed that most papers on the Copper Scrolls don't even mention it at all."

"Is that what we are looking for?"

Naamah, ignoring her companion's questions, leaned over the eighth column again and began to read out loud. "A bar of silver, ten vessels of offering, and ten books are in the aqueduct on the road that is to the east of Bet Ahsor, which is east of Ahzor."

"Ten books?" Atticus asked, puzzled.

Naamah laughed again, her eyes dancing with flame. Her stare was so intense he had to avert his eyes.

"That is where the fools made their error," she said, grabbing Atticus by his collar and pulling him against her body. It was warm and soft, and even though she was borne of Hell, smelled heavenly. "Look," she instructed, pointing at a series of characters.

"The characters here are worn and faded, and only 'A S A R' can be made out. The researchers who deciphered this were forced to take many liberties due to the abundance of missing letters and whole words due to the passage of time."

Atticus shook his head. He was focused and he understood.

"So, they had 'Book' clear and 'A S A R.' The ancient Hebrew word for ten is A S A R A, so they agreed the word was ten and that an 'A' was missing. However, I know the book I seek, and I also know the proper translation of 'A S A R' is

'B A S A R.'" She paused and looked up at Atticus.

"And what does 'basar' mean in ancient Hebrew?"

"Flesh," she said, running her pink, wet tongue over her lips. "'The Book of Flesh' - the real treasure of the Copper Scroll, and the only object the ancients were trying to hide. Everything else in the treasure list was a ruse."

"Does it say who they were hiding it from?"

"Well, that's an easy question." She smiled, then rubbed and tapped his muscular chest. "They were hiding the book from Solomon himself."

"I don't follow," he sputtered.

"The ancient priests knew that anyone who possessed both the Ring Seal of Solomon and The Book of Flesh would be unstoppable - the ruler of all, above and below."

"My ring?" Atticus asked, his interest supremely piqued.

"Our ring," she corrected through squinted eyes.

"I didn't mean it like that," he said, shifting. "I meant 'mine' like the ring I found in the old book shop."

"Relax," she said, smirking. "I know you would never dream of betraying me."

"Never," he repeated. This time it was he that grabbed her hips and pulled her close to him. He couldn't take it anymore. He needed to kiss this new rendition of Jade. "I wouldn't even know where to begin."

The she-demon relaxed her tension a hair and let her body come to his. They kissed a long passionate kiss that was broken by a massive explosion just beyond the hole in the wall behind them. Smoke and acrid bands of sulfur bellowed into their space, driven by the force of an incendiary device that had just been detonated. It was to no avail, of course. Asmodeus could not be harmed by man's artillery.

"Come," she instructed. "We are almost done here, and they are growing closer." Reaching out, she tapped her long black fingernail on the glass panel covering the column eight text. It was such a soft tap that Atticus wasn't even sure she had made contact. When the glass spidered and split, however, melting into a fine dust, he stopped questioning her actions any further. Naamah leaned forward, pouted her lips, and with a puff of supernatural-fueled air, blew the dust from the case, leaving the scroll section exposed to the air and her fingers. Plucking it gently from its velvet lined bed, she placed the delicate fragment into the palm of her hand.

"You will have mere seconds to record what I bring to light," Naamah said, her voice serious as death. Atticus knew she was depending on him here. "I am going to warm the copper with the fires and heat of Hell. You must record what you see, understood?"

"Understood." He moved into position as Naamah began to chant and vibrate the metal shard in her hands.

Gunshots ripped through the opening in the wall. The splintering and shattering of tile and plaster had no impact on Naamah, and she continued her conjuring. Atticus followed suit, and ignoring the ramparts to their rear, he snatched a pad and pencil from the security desk and readied himself for whatever she was going to reveal.

"Be ready," she cried out, as her body suddenly tensed as if stricken with agony. Atticus watched as the scroll fragment begin to glow. The metal became an amber or orange hue at first, before giving way to an intensifying, glowing red.

"Now!" she cried. "You will have but a moment to record the map before the copper is turned to dust!"

Peering down and focusing on her hands, Atticus was awe-struck as lines and curves began to trace themselves in deep, glowing red across the surface of the metal sheet. Putting pencil to paper, he began to sketch what he saw.

"Take a picture!" Naamah commanded, her face alive with pain and ecstasy. "It will last longer, for fuck's sake."

31

Alexander turned the ancient brass skeleton key and listened as the chambers rose and fell, locking the solid oak door to his private study. Dropping the key into the breast pocket of his jacket, he turned to face the raging fire Philip had prepared for him. He watched as the embers danced and licked at the air above, reaching for some invisible source of fuel - of some fodder to keep itself alive. It was always searching, grasping, twisting and turning for the next piece of matter to consume. Alive. The unsuspecting flames seemingly unaware of their byproduct... light. This ignorance must surely be so, for the deeds the flames chased seemed more aptly situated to the darkness. Turning life to ash, complex structures to blocks of spent carbon - this was not the work of the light. And yet wherever the insatiable flames moved - there was light.

Alexander stepped to his richly adorned reader chair, a masterpiece of wood and leather, and settled himself in. Lifting a glass of port his shuffling sage had poured for him, he sniffed, then sipped. The old goat was always attempting to get Alexander to partake in one libation or another. To what end he did not know, nor did he really care. He was simply making an observation to bide his time. He had no idea of the schedule of demons and did not know if she would come at all, let alone this evening. Alex did, however, trust in the abilities of Asar - not to be persuasive, per se, or to get any one task done. No, he trusted in Asar to complete any undertaking Alexander asked of him. That is where his skill set lay. Loyal perseverance to the end defined him, and they were both fine with this.

Alexander took another swig of the smoky-sweet wine and placed the empty glass on the circular table at his side. Stretching a bit, he shifted and found comfort in the big-backed chair. His eyes returned to the fire. The flames caught sight of him and began a private, mesmerizing display. He felt his eyes grow heavy and thought about calling it a night, when he uncontrollably drifted off to the refuge of the land of dreams.

"Pilgrim..." a soft, seductive voice whispered into his ear. Her mouth was so close that Alexander felt the brush of her lips disturb the fine hairs of his lobe. His eyes shot open, and he found her before him.

"Morning, sleepy head," she purred. Bathin was sprawled out on the love seat opposite his chair. Her head rested on her elbow, which rested on an arm of the couch. Her body was spread out across the couch, with her long, inviting legs exposed to the flickering flames. She wore a gauze-like white linen robe, which allowed Alexander to view every line and curve of her body below.

"Sorry to wake you, Alexander Storm," she laughed playfully, tossing her long silken auburn hair about in a teasing motion. "But a fat Egyptian bird said you needed to see me."

Alexander caught his bearings, which had been floating somewhere between sleep and Bathin's nude body. Sitting upright, he smiled an awkward smile at his guest.

"Thank you for coming, Bathin... I am well aware of the risk you have assumed."

"Oh stop," she said, sitting upright on the loveseat and slowly drawing her knees apart. The fireplace's flames jumped and nipped at the site of her womanly regions. Alex, unable to avert his eyes before catching sight of her, felt an odd blush take him.

"When Alexander Storm tells a girl to come... she cums," she said, laughing infectiously at her own humor.

"You always were a barrel of wit." Alexander spoke without malice, and she recognized she was truly in a territorial truce for the moment.

"You know how I feel about you, Storm." She looked at him seriously now, "But I am not comfortable spending one more moment than I need to here... in the castle... at Dragon Loch. Bad mojo for my kind."

"Understood." He nodded and rose to his feet. Walking past the couch, he stopped at the back of the seat and peered down at her. She remained locked on the chair he had just vacated.

"I have a few questions." He spoke quickly now, as something was unnerving him. He couldn't put his finger on it, but it was predicated on that stare.

"Fire away..." she replied.

"If you answer truthfully, I will grant you a temporary hiatus... a vacation from my involvement in your... existence."

"Agreed..." she said. She was still locked on the chair. What was it?

"Excellent," he began. "First and foremost, how did you escape the... ahh... heavenly altitudes we ported to?"

She laughed. "Well, that's a doozy to start with."

"Really?"

"Well, the fact of it is I don't really know... I just knew I had my portal ability... it had been returned to me."

"I see." Alexander pondered her answer and nodded his head. "So did you portal only yourself out?"

"No, you silly pilgrim." Her head snapped to him, and her features were darker now, malice alighting in her eyes. "There were three... including me."

Alexander's eyes closed tightly at the revelation.

"Naamah?"

"Mmm-hmm," she said, giggling now. The fire was dying. Alexander spun to his left. There was a sound of breathing... no, wet slurping. He couldn't place it. Bathin remained in his sight in front of him.

"Who else did you pluck from the stars, Bathin? Who else did you deliver to Earth?" A chill ran down the length of his spine as the words left his mouth.

"YOU!" She cried in his ear. He jumped and stumbled. The fire died. Darkness took the room.

"You... you... you..." The voices came from all around him. "You begged me to take you from that place. You granted me my new stones, Storm. You know that. Only a previous master of the stones can issue stones anew. You... why do you have a dead body in your tower? You, Storm... you unleashed me back on Earth... you released Naamah... you... all YOU!"

Silence filled the darkness. The fire went red, and the flames spread through the hearth once again, illuminating the room. It was empty. The demon was gone.

Alexander brushed his jacket sleeves in a symbolic dusting and withdrew the ancient key from his pocket. He had planned well for her visit. Her likeness still on the couch had been an illusion. She had been up and about the room looking for an exit into the castle - most likely to possess one of his unsuspecting guests. The room was sealed up tight and the dragon lock had safeguarded the door against her exit.

He inserted the key now and spun to disengage the lock. Stepping into the hall, he shut the door behind him as one final chill rippled down his spine.

32

"Alexander!" Kate cried out, chasing him down the long corridor to the library. "Alexander!"

Stopping in his tracks, he took a deep breath and spun to face Kate. Smiling, he offered her a tap on the back as she worked to catch her breath.

"All right my dear, all right."

"It's... not... all right," she finally got out, pulling a folded paper from her back pocket. She shoved it at him while she partook in a few more deep medicinal inhales.

"What's this?" Alexander asked as he unfolded the pages. "What is this about, Kate?"

"Look," she instructed him. "Is this what you've been looking for? A bloodbath and theft at the Jordanian Museum!" she shouted. "There are reports of sorcery and a man and a woman infiltrating the inner sanctum of the museum."

Alexander read on as Kate fiddled around him, adrenaline coursing through her veins.

Alexander looked up, "The Copper Scroll..." he said. It was a statement, not a question.

"I know!" she exclaimed. "Can you believe this? Is it what you were looking for?"

"Yes," he finally answered. "I believe it is... assemble everyone in the dining hall... thirty minutes."

Kate nodded and was gone. Alex continued on his path to the library and quickly perused a few volumes before heading to the hall himself.

"DUE TO RECENT EVENTS," Alexander said, addressing his guests, "we need to split into three groups and head to the Holy Land."

There were a series of odd noises which surely represented some guttural form of dislike. Alexander surmised it was due to the splitting of the group. None of them liked it, but it was often the only way to cover enough ground.

"Kate," he began. "You, Abigail and Samantha will come with me to Qumran."

"Qum-what?" Sam asked on cue.

"Qumran," Alexander replied sharply. "The desert caves in which the Dead Sea Scrolls were found. We will head there."

"Why Qumran, Alex?" Serket inquired.

"Someone stole the Copper Scroll yesterday, right out of the museum."

"The Copper Scroll!" Anika and Serket exclaimed in unison.

"Yes, and there is only one reason to take the Copper Scroll." Ever the professor, Alexander scanned the room. "A good old fashioned..."

"Treasure hunt," Anika finished.

"Exactly," Serket said, joining in the assumption.

Alexander nodded. "Treasure hunt. Serket, you and Anika are going to head to Qumran with us, however, you will immediately depart to join up with..."

"Don't you say it Storm," Serket said, rising from her seat. "I just got a premonition... don't you dare say..."

"Jericho." Alexander finished.

"Damn it all to hell." Serket threw a very quiet, very modest tantrum and returned to her seat.

"I thought you two found a common ground on our last outing?"

"I thought so too," she replied dryly. "Then he made a few comments right before his departure which put him back in the same light, as far as I am concerned."

Alexander nodded sympathetically, walking in her direction. "I understand," he offered. "But beneath all that, Francis is a good man... I need you to work with him here... it is unavoidable. He will require your talents before the day is through."

"Really," she said, looking at him. "Exactly which talents are those?"

"Hunter... wolf and..." Alex lowered his voice to almost a whisper. "Black magic witch."

Serket said nothing. Her eyes transmitted both understanding and compliance in his wishes.

"What of William and company?" Anika questioned, noticing Alexander gathering to leave.

"Oh, yes." Alexander turned and smiled. "Asar, Keith and William Decker will also be in the Holy Land. However, they will be there to commit a very challenging burglary at the Research Institute on the regional campus."

"Huh?"

"I will explain in a bit more detail once we are underway," Alex promised, taking Anika by the shoulder. "Pack light," he reminded the group. "Thirty minutes, on the roof."

And he was gone.

33

Frank Jericho pushed open the heavy wooden doors that barred entry to small village's pub. The force it took to move the massive, hinged panels was no accident. Children, and probably woman for that matter, were not at the top of this watering hole's guest list.

Frank's eyes took a minute to adjust to the dimly lit, archaic infrastructure of the tavern. After peering into the white-hot snow drifts for the past four hours, he would need more than a moment to become accustomed to the light, or lack thereof.

Making out the outlines of a bar and stools ahead of him, he made his way forward and leaned on the countertop. Blinking a few times, his vision began to soften.

"Here."

The rough voice of the barkeep shocked him, although he betrayed nothing on the exterior. Homicide detective... streets of NYC... mask your feelings and become tough as nails... or wither and die.

"Thanks," Frank managed, reaching for the glass and missing. The cool surface of the shot slid into his hand.

"It'll blind you," the barkeep offered, "but only temporary, y'see... or you will. Drink."

"Thanks." Jericho was genuinely appreciative. Bringing the glass to his lips, he poured and swallowed in one smooth, practiced move. About five seconds after drinking the concoction, he felt the liquid magma stir at the bottom of his chest. Fighting back a cough, he morphed it into speech. "Another."

"Ha!" The barkeep celebrated Jericho's prowess and the entire bar came to life. "He's fine, boys," he instructed the rest of the patrons, who were just now coming into focus. And there were plenty, at that. The saloon, aptly known as Wolf's Bane and Moon Dust, currently housed over fifty or sixty customers.

The bartender slid the second shot to Frank, who lifted it and hit it smooth and hard again, resulting in a second cheer.

"How's ya eyes now, stranger?"

"Good enough to see how ugly you are..." Frank said, taking a chance. The man stared at him with anger brewing in his ruddy, bearded brow. *Ugh.* Frank thought, *I was doing so well.*

"HAAA!" The bartender couldn't hold it anymore, letting out a loud jovial burst at Jericho's wise-assery.

"Sup?" the man asked.

"Sure," Jericho said, smiling and starving.

"Good. Just put up lamb stew this morn. Go grab the table with them there... they're clearly your lasses... and I bring ya out."

Frank slid from the high stool and walked further into the bar. He spotted Anika waving to him and Serket averting her face. He laughed.

"Ladies," he said, pulling out a chair and sitting.

Serket's animal-lined hood was pulled tight over her face and only her deep-set eyes reflected in the inner darkness. She stared out at Jericho.

"So, you guys come here often?" he said, trying to break the ice to no avail.

"Get serious," Serket hissed at him. "This is deathly serious..."

"I know, I'm sorry..." he offered. "Just trying to break the tension."

Serket sat forward now, pulling her hood back and exposing her warrior face.

"Well, don't. Leave the tension. We are about to ruin these poor people's lives and will be lucky to keep our own hides by the end."

Jericho looked around briefly and signaled her to settle down. "I get it... sorry."

"Don't be sorry," she chided, rising from her chair. "Eat your damn stew and let's get on with it... we must be done before the darkness takes the day."

34

Atticus gazed longingly at the perfect feminine shape of Naamah. She was several strident steps ahead of him and the intensifying rays of the setting sun bombarded her body. The long, ultra-thin linen robe she wore worked as a cinema screen, and coupled with the solar lighting, created a flawless silhouette of her body within. On the rest of her body were several loose hanging bracelets and a wonderfully rugged pair of hiking or work boots.

Atticus remained steadfast in his position for several minutes, enjoying the view and wondering where exactly they were headed. He had researched the two city names provided in the Copper Scroll's translation, or at least he had Googled them, and there were no results. Zero. No mention in ancient atlases, historical accountings, or religious texts. The cities of Bet Ahsor and Ahzor never existed, by all accounts. He had even had the foresight to play around with the letters, kind of like the jumble word game in the Sunday Post he loved to play. Nothing. No combination of the letters resulted in anything resembling a geographic location or a city name. So honestly, even though the view was stupendous, what the hell were they doing marching out into this no man's land at nightfall?

“Your eyes tired yet?” Naamah called from ahead.

“Huh?” he replied. He was caught off-guard and knocked from his train of thought.

“Get up here, you foolish boy,” she said, stopping as he jogged to meet her.

“That’s a great robe,” he noted with a smile, reaching her in a sprint.

“Enough games.” She was facing the sky, tracing the constellations. “We have serious work to do. And if we do not successfully complete our tasks,” she said, eying him, “you don’t get to play with what’s under the robe.” She paused for effect. “Got it?”

“Yup,” he replied, stepping in front of Naamah, impeding her forward progress. “I get it. Quick question… where are we going?”

Naamah shook her head in annoyance. Hadn’t he been listening? Sometimes she questioned his usefulness. He had come through in some clutch situations leading up this, but nothing that would have altered her getting here. She liked the companionship and the sex, but honestly, she could grab any lad to satisfy these needs. So why?

“Have you so soon forgotten the words of the Scroll?” she posited dryly.

He shook his head, “I didn’t forget anything. In fact, while we were headed here, I took the opportunity to scour the Web. There is not one solitary mention of either of the places the Scroll refers to. That’s why I am truly concerned as to where we are headed.”

“Really?” Naamah seemed impressed by his initiative, at least. “Nothing, huh?”

“That’s right.” His face wore sentiments of hurt and confusion. “So why are you leading me out to the desert?”

"Leading you to the desert?” she said, sputtering the words. “Oh honey, if I wanted to be rid of you I would do it when and where the urge struck me.”

He considered this statement and realized she was probably telling the truth in this regard.

“Fine.” He pivoted to her side so that she could proceed. “Then do you mind filling me in?”

"Of course," she said, smiling a foxlike grin. "But we must talk and walk. You okay with that?"

He nodded and she continued.

"So, you searched for the cities of Bet Ahsor and Ahzor, is that right?"

"Yes." He had to double step to keep pace. Her long legs seemed to move effortlessly through the soft sand.

"You found no results because these are not the names of any cities of man."

He looked at her with a puzzled expression. "I don't follow."

"These names refer to cities of the jinn. There..." she said, pointing to a large cluster of rock and sand. Turning, she headed into the dying light.

"The Ifrit, to be exact. Sort of long-lost cousins of mine. The cities of Bet Ahsor and Ahzor refer to a world hidden from the eyes of mortals - of pigs and men."

"Hey," he said, objecting to the characterization.

"Did you not just spend the better part of an hour staring at the outline of my body and imagining all the debaucherous things you would do to it once you got a chance?"

He scratched his head. "Yeah, okay... point taken."

Naamah reached the rock formation and searched along the base of the largest blocks of sandstone. Running her finger just below the sand line, she began to trace something hidden by the timeless granules of dust and dirt.

"This will do," she announced. Rising upright, she undid the strap that held her robe in place and slid the linen off her shoulders, allowing it to drop to the desert floor. Atticus's eyes grew wide at the sight of her naked body, shadowed by the twilight of the disappearing sun in the back and illuminated by the ivory sphere of the moon in the front. She was a splendid sight - naked in the vicious desert land, save her boots of course, and exposed for all to see.

Dropping to her knees in the sand, she spoke without turning. "And how does one find a jinn city, you may ask?" Spreading her arms out, then over her head, she stretched towards the heavens and reached as she bowed to the floor of the desert.

"You summon a jinn for directions, of course," she hissed, as her body went into a tantric state. She began rising and falling to the earth. Her lips moved, and a chant followed their movement a moment behind in time. Over and over she performed this ritual, and Atticus stood, silent and mesmerized by the display. Her movements and the fervor of her chant expounded to animal levels. Her feet dug further into the sand until the cheeks of her ass were obfuscated by the desert as well.

A sudden, wretched stink filled the air, and Atticus reacted and recoiled, covering his mouth and nose with a hack. Regaining his composure, he noticed the bead of a small flame had ignited upon the top of the largest of stones. Circular smoke soon danced a purposeful course of design atop the stone, and the flame intensified. Naamah's chaotic ritual continued intensifying yet again. Atticus became fearful for the very structure of her body. Her skin, muscles, and hair moved in a rapidly violent fashion, snapping and yanking. He was sure he was about to see her come apart in front of his eyes.

Atticus took several steps towards her visually morphing body, thought better of it, stopped, and then experienced such an intense heat flash, he was thrown back and to the ground by the sheer kinetic brilliance of the light upon the stone.

Lifting his head and peering across his body, he saw Naamah, still and silent. She appeared to be intact and out of the harm's way. His eyes followed her gaze to the stone altar, where he found a monstrous winged creature perched. Its red eyes cut through the moonlit night and fixed on him.

The creature launched itself from the stone and landed over Atticus. The acrid odors of Hell exuded from the creature's lungs, and it lowered its face within inches of his own, spewing forth stink and vileness on his face. Its eyes bulged as it brought a great arm up and over its body, forking its taloned fingers forward. Atticus realized he was about to be torn to pieces.

"Belial..." Naamah had risen and was facing them now. "Belial, it is I, your sister, Naamah," she bellowed into the desert night. The demon spun to face her, its eyes studying her nude form and analyzing her eyes and her scent.

"The human is mine, and I would appreciate it if you would leave him intact." She took several steps towards them now. "He still holds value and purpose to me."

"Sister..." the ancient beast finally spoke, "is it you who have summoned me?"

"Indeed, oh mighty warrior." She smiled and ran her hand across Belial's massive, blackened chest. "I find myself in need of a jinn's knowledge, and I thought who better to call upon then my dear friend."

"I have not heard from you in a millennium, witch," he grunted. "Why would I help you... *dear friend.*"

"Well," she said as she walked to Atticus and extended him a hand, her nude body still exciting him amidst the imminent danger that was Balial. "I call on you concerning a common enemy... a common cause."

"Speak," he demanded. "You have summoned me to this forsaken place... now speak or I will make my exit from this realm."

"Alexander Storm."

The words rattled through the air and wormed their way with a powerful punch into the demon's ears.

"Storm..." he growled.

"Storm, yes... and he is coming. He is coming for Atticus and me. We have formulated and set a trap, however."

Naamah let the archaic evil consider her words a moment as she returned to Atticus. Embracing him in her naked form, she ran a hand down and into his pant pocket, extracting the leather pouch he kept there. Looking into Atticus' eyes, she instructed him to remain silent with her gaze.

"I possess a most powerful weapon, my lord." She laughed and spilled the contents of the pouch into the palm of her hand. Holding her arm out, she implored Balial to look.

The Ifrit roared with recognition at the sight of the ring.

"Where did you get that?" it hollered. "Where did you find Solomon's curse?"

Holding the ring between both of her hands, she wiggled ever so slightly, like a child. "I took it from DeMolay's corpse when I took the life of the last Templar Knight."

Belial smiled at her words. "The Templar Grand Master rots?"

"He does."

"You have been a busy witch, Naamah," the archaic demon said, laughing. "What do you need from me?"

Finally. Naamah smiled and spoke. "Bet Ahsor and Ahzor?"

"What about them," he puzzled. "They are cities of the jinn."

"They are part of an ancient riddle, and I must solve this riddle in order to get a final, all-powerful weapon to destroy Storm, Dragon Loch, and retroactively abort his entire lineage."

The demon nodded in understanding.

"All right." He smiled now. "Tell me the exact passage."

Naamah cleared her throat and lifted her chest in mocking theatrics.

"A bar of silver, ten vessels of offering, and ten books are in the aqueduct on the road that is to the east of Bet Ahsor, which is east of Ahzor."

"Ha!" Belial called out. "That is quite simple, Naamah."

"You are great and wise, cousin." She was laying it on now. "Surely you can now see why we required your assistance."

"Clearly," he replied with great torrents of pride.

"Can you lead us there?" she asked. "I must have access to the treasure before Storm."

"Of course." The demon pointed ahead of them into the heat-diffusing landscape of the desert. "It is not far from where we stand."

Pleased, Naamah bowed and thanked the jinn.

"Not that I don't enjoy your current state," Balial said, smiling. "But may I suggest you cover yourself before we pass through Bet Ahsor - otherwise, my brothers there will ravish your body beyond your wildest imagination, as they will be unable to control themselves."

Naamah was in the process of retrieving her robe from the desert floor as Belial offered his warning.

"Oh, my." She laughed, throwing her robe over her shoulder and out of sight. "What's a girl to do?"

35

Alexander Storm stepped from the military transport vehicle into the sweltering heat of the Qumran desert. Shielding his eyes with his hand turned sideways, he scanned the hills, caves and small mountains that lay before him.

"Welcome to Qumran, ladies," he said as they departed the vehicle.

"Looks like a blast." Samantha was in her normal form, at last.

"Amazing," Kate uttered as she burst free of the confines of the motorcade and sprinted out into the open desert. She peered up at the speckled openings in the high hills. They had reached the sacred caves she had read so much about - the resting place for the Dead Sea Scrolls... what else could be more exciting?

"Gives me a bit of a chill," Abigail spoke sharply. Alex turned to her.

"A chill?" he questioned. "It's quite stifling here, my dear."

Walking towards Kate, Abigail brushed past Alexander. "Yes, I know. That's what makes me nervous, Mr. Storm."

"Alex," he quickly interjected.

"Huh?"

"Alex, Abigail. Alex or Alexander is more than sufficient. We have known each other for a spell now and shared much in a short period of time. Enough with the Mr. Storm, okay?"

Abi smiled and nodded.

"What do you feel, exactly?" Alex inquired. "You need to hone these skills. Recognize signs - recognize your gut... your instincts."

"I don't know how to put it into words," she said, and moaned at some unforeseen force that was oppressing her. "Desolate... hopeless... endless... time... BLOOD!"

Alexander jumped at the sharp change in tone. Running to Abigail's side, he embraced her.

"Hey," he inquired demandingly. "What happened? What did you see?"

She sunk her head into his warm chest. He smelled of amber and bergamot. Her head began to swirl.

"What did you see, Abigail," Alexander whispered. "Tell me... share the burden."

She thought for a moment, still engaged in the embrace and unsure if sharing was the answer.

"Please," Storm implored again, causing her to loosen her grasp on him and step back.

"Fine," she sighed, "I saw the sand amongst these ruins... these caves, drenched in the sticky hot mess of blood, coming straight up to the castle walls." She trembled as she spoke. "Something you brought to Dragon Loch, something you will bring... will be the end of us all, Alexander."

A chill ran down his spine as he stared into the young girl's eyes.

"Mr. Storm," a voice called from the passenger seat of the transport. "Mr. Storm, we've got something."

Alexander and Abigail made their way around to the passenger side door and found a camouflaged soldier with one leg stretched out on the edge of the open door frame, computer tablet in hand.

"What did you find?" Alexander inquired, then turned to Abi. "They've got drones in the air combing every inch of Qumran and a bit beyond."

Abigail nodded and looked at the screen.

"See these markers here?" The soldier pointed to several pulsing blips on the screen. "They represent movement with a body mass beyond that of the largest animal that inhabits these regions."

"So, it can only be... ugh..." Alex cleared his throat. "Human."

"Correct," the soldier said, nodding. "These are your birds... nobody out here... not this far."

Alexander nodded and excused himself for a moment. Walking to the front of the vehicle, he peered over the hood into the landscape before him. Kate was walking about a hundred yards out, stopping every few seconds to bend and pick up some piece of debris from the ground. Lifting it to her eyes, she would examine it briefly, then drop it back to the ground. Alex watched in innocent appreciation as she searched the ancient soil for a trinket or artifact she could collect. Samantha, on the other hand, was traveling several steps behind Kate, her head and hands moving in all directions - driving Kate mad, he had no doubt. She was likely complaining about Alex, about the heat, the dirt, the plan, and anything else she couldn't control. He gave them a moment more. They were about to be stripped of another layer of innocence this afternoon - he had no doubt. Best let them explore a bit and enjoy the desert - before they grew to fear it.

Samantha was shouting to Kate. He could hear something but could not make out the words. Here in the desert, amongst the Dead Sea Caves, sound seemed to stop and experience absorption at a startling rate.

"What is it?" Abigail had joined him.

"Not sure," Alex replied, without taking his eyes off the girls. "Kate was doing a bit of surface archaeology, to no avail. Something caught Sam's attention on the ground, I believe, and she summoned Kate over." Alexander made his way to the other side of the transport.

"Kate!" he yelled, "Sam... head back now, please."

They were involved with whatever they had found, and either didn't hear the calls or were ignoring them as they were concentrating.

"Hey!" Alexander shouted again, waving them in. They still didn't look up.

Alex drew a breath and meant to scream even louder when Abigail cut him off with a shrill, double-fisted whistle.

"Samantha!" she shouted. "Kate!" They looked up to see Abigail waving them in.

"Very good," Alexander said, nodding. "You will have to teach me how to do that."

"Whistle?" Abi laughed.

"No... I can whistle," he replied and began to belt out a concerto of one classic or another. Pausing his tune, he added, "That's whistling... I want you to teach me that air raid siren technique."

She smiled as Kate and Sam walked around the truck. "Sure thing, Alex... I will teach you."

"Alexander," Kate huffed. "Check it out!" She held out her palm.

Alex appraised the artifact in her hand. "What a splendid specimen of a Hebrew oil lamp, Kate. Congratulations!"

She smiled, absorbing the praise for a moment, then added, "Sam actually spotted it... I walked right past it."

"Oh stop," Sam said, grimacing. "You could have taken credit. I could care less, dude."

"Well, teamwork then, I guess," Abi interjected, and Alexander nodded in agreement.

Suddenly a din of radios broke out. There was shouting back and forth, and the driver and passenger were carrying on separate radio conversations.

"Mr. Storm?" The driver stuck his head out the window. "Those are your inbounds... I've parsed the crew your objective coordinates from the drone scan data."

Alexander Storm acknowledged the soldier's statement and pointed towards the incoming choppers. The passenger soldier rose from his seat. Standing on the inner edge of the door, he was able to peer over the top of the cab and see Storm and the girls.

"There has been some kind of incident at the Israel Antiquities Authority campus storage unit or something!" he yelled. "Central Command requires our return to assist."

Alexander nodded. "Sounds serious," he said, and turned to the girls. "Any casualties or injured?"

"I dunno," the soldier said sharply, shifting the vehicle into drive. "Sounds like a crazy scene, though."

"Well, Godspeed then." Storm waved them on. "Thanks for your help. We have it from here."

The soldier saluted and the transport kicked plumes of dust and rubble as it peeled from the Qumran ruins and sped back to Jerusalem at breakneck speeds.

As quickly as the vehicle's dust faded, it began to churn up again, a slave to the incoming chopper's whirling blades.

"Cover your mouth and eyes," Alexander called out as the copter set down. "Quickly, he called to them! Get on."

Once safely in the air, Samantha caught Alexander's attention, who nodded to her. "Looks like the boys are wreaking havoc in Jerusalem," she said.

"It would appear so, Sam." He frowned ever so slightly, but she caught it. "I just hope they are long gone with their objectives."

"As long as they got out," she said, nodding. "We can always go back for what you need. There will be another chance."

"Sadly."

Alex peered at Samantha with piercing eyes, and a chill ran down her neck. *Oh shit*, she thought to herself, *I fucking missed something here.*

"Sadly," he repeated. "If they have not been successful in their endeavors, I fear there will *not* be another chance."

"What the hell, Storm?" She shifted in her seat as the momentary peace she had just experienced with Kate was ripped from her soul. "Are we at DEFCON 20 already?" How did the level of threat slip by her? She could read his eyes even better now - they said *shut up, Sam.*

Sitting back in her seat on the chopper, Samantha gazed out the window at the landscape whizzing by in a blur. She then turned and looked at Kate and Abigail, who remained oblivious to the seriousness of their situation. *Good*, she thought, *let's keep it like that.*

"I wish Lobo was here," she whispered to Alexander.

"So do I, my dear Samantha. So do I."

Alexander extended an arm around her shoulder and pulled Sam to the safety of his side chest. Samantha did not resist.

36

The unfamiliar sound of gunfire filled the grounds surrounding the Jay and Jeanie Schottenstein National Campus' climate-controlled storage facility in Jerusalem.

Only a few weeks earlier, this very facility had been the backdrop for news reports from every nation on the planet. A discovery in one of the caves by the Dead Sea became international news and had spread like wildfire across the globe. Four silver swords in pristine condition had been recovered from a cave. The timing was odd, as the site was being surveyed as part of a student study project. The Cave, as it was now known, had been explored dozens of times over the past few decades without anything of value being pulled from its recesses in the past. Now, when the discovery was apparently needed, the swords appeared.

When discussing the situation with Decker and Asar via telephone, Alexander Storm had very nonchalantly stated that "the swords were NOT in the cave... until they *needed* to be in the cave." What did that mean? Alexander Storm's thought process did not align with the rest of humanity. He was hundreds of moves ahead of the curve at any moment.

"I need the swords," he told them. "The swords know that. Go to them and they will come to you to be brought to me."

"What?" Decker had demanded more information. Asar had scoffed, but would always follow Alexander's instructions.

The cache of silver swords was engraved in a language that apparently no one could identify. This was an interesting tidbit that had been withheld. With the rest of the world eating, sleeping, working, making love, and everything else they do in a day, clueless to what is truly occurring around them, essentially one man, with some assistance from a small group of confidants, was able to keep the end at bay, chase the wolf from the door, and conquer the boogeyman as junior slept with his teddy, safe and sound.

The news did catch wind of the stalactite the weapons were found behind. It seemed there was an engraving on the hanging stone marker. That much was reported. How about an image of the marker text? What language was it in? What did it say? Apparently, no one knew that either. Storm had reached out, but no one knew what the text said. Didn't anyone find that odd? No one could email him a photograph or a roughing. Also, quite odd, no?

But Alexander Storm knew before anyone else would or could that he needed the Four Swords, or else. He needed the Four Swords, forged in an ancient unknown alloy, not silver, as reported. *He needed them. He knew this.* The Four Swords' time had come - which also meant whatever the Four Swords were forged to kill - that thing's time had come too, right?

The Four Swords' time had come - and thank God for that! Thank God for the existence of whatever Evil they were forged to kill. For without that Evil, the Four Swords would not have been needed. And if they weren't needed, Asar, Keith, and William Decker would not have experienced what could only be labeled intervention, divine or otherwise. Alexander Storm needed the Four Swords. Something was coming. And because of this, Asar, Keith, and Decker emerged from an onslaught of gunfire, explosive devices, tank fire, and a cellulose bomb detonated on them in the facility that was designed to be a last resort method to stop the removal of the Four Swords. A nuclear option. Who makes a nuclear option to protect four artifacts?

They emerged without a scratch, climbing into their ancient, beat-to-crap van - the one with the little vagabond girl sleeping in the back, waiting for them - and they drove away. The Four Swords were on their way to Alexander Storm... because he needed them... now!

37

Alerik threw the truck into drive and blasted through the overgrown foliage that had developed into natural camouflage. The road was seldom traveled on foot, let alone with a vehicle. Jericho leaned and surveyed his companions in the back seat. Their faces looked tired, and their cold noses and bloodshot eyes made them look like a couple of twins.

"You ladies all right back there?" he asked, already knowing the response. They were both headstrong warrior stock. They were not about to betray their steely exterior with feminine stereotypes. *So much so*, he thought, *that they're probably not even considering their behavior, or how not to appear weaker or less sturdy than men*.

When a woman was of their caliber, there was no masquerade. What you saw was what you got - the hard with the soft, the vicious with the beautiful, the passionate love with the all-consuming capacity for hate. Anika and Serket were equal pictures of womanly perfection in his eyes - although, he would never, could never, let either of them know. He knew, and that was enough. He would lay down his life tonight, or any other moment in time for either of them. Likewise, he was pretty sure they would reciprocate that sentiment if necessary. And also likewise, neither would ever admit that in the light of day.

"All good," he said, nodding at their silence.

Anika smiled. "Would rather be elsewhere," she whispered.

"Understood." Frank turned to look out the windshield. He was not expecting a response from the scorpion woman.

"And if I'm going to be honest with you," he said, still facing forward. "I've done my share of shit for Storm over the years. This little excursion falls under the heading of being the biggest possible clusterfuck of 'em all."

Silence filled the truck as the wicked landscape of the forest flew by in green and brown blurs. Jericho checked his watch - actually his father's watch originally, but his now. He flashed back to an odd and disturbing memory of his pop, emaciated and wasting away in the hospice bed. The smells, the desolation, the reaper round every corner of the dimly lit facility. He and his dad had a tumultuous relationship through the years, and there had been long spans of time without any contact at all. The years... all those wasted years. Since his father's passing, he had privately wept over that notion of wasted time on more than one occasion. But there, in the cold, unfamiliar hospice bed, lying in the growing shadow of death, Jericho had found all the time in the world for their relationship.

What a fucking waste.

That last night was filled with convulsions and pain. Empty, clueless eyes stared up at him most of the time. His father's mouth was always slightly ajar, with the foul stench of the demon cancer emanating from deep within him. There was however, that short moment of time, that last night, when his father was with him. His deep brown eyes, full of compassion and unconditional love, spoke volumes of apologies and regret. They had talked softly to each other, relaying memories of youth and high energy days of activities and family events.

Life... they spoke of life.

Shortly before leaving Francis for the last time, his father had summoned enough strength to unbuckle his watch and slide it into his son's hand. It was the silly watch his father took such pride in, a Doxa SUB 300 Searambler - a diver's watch. His father had spun many a tale which started with a glance at the face of that watch first. He relished in discussing the groundbreaking technology this watch had introduced.

What the hell was it, he thought to himself while speeding along into the shadows of doom, mesmerized by the lull of the truck's engine and the streaks of green foliage. *HRR, or HV?* No, it flew back into his mind's eye like the rush of a waterfall. *Helium release valve... HVR.*

It was a big deal for divers, and this small underdog of a company had beat out the big boys, like Rolex, to get it to market first. It had offered a tremendous advance in oxygen monitoring and depth tracking precision for scuba divers and had led the way for a domino effect of advanced technology in the market. Frank Jericho's dad never did go scuba diving, though. He did, however, smoke two packs of cigarettes a day.

"Jericho."

He snapped to attention at the sound of Anika's voice and found her holding her cell's screen to face him. He squinted, nodded, and directed his attention to the driver.

"Alerik."

The driver nodded in response.

"Mr. Storm sent coordinates - you got something to plug 'em in to?"

The driver remained stoic as he maneuvered the treacherous terrain.

"Alerik?"

"No need," the driver said. His thick, baroque Eastern European accent filled the truck's interior, and Serket raised an eyebrow in surprise. "I know where the Baba Yaga dwells."

"Baba Yaga?!" Anika shot up in her seat. "What is he talking about, Jericho?"

"Yes, Francis," said Serket. *Ahh, the Scorpion speaks.* "What about the Baba Yaga?"

Serket and Anika shifted in their seats and shimmied closer to the front of the truck. Jericho, recognizing the need to stem a mutiny, spun to face the pair.

"Our mission," he started, but was quickly shut down by Serket.

"We know our mission," Serket said. She was all business. "Enter an ancient cemetery. Locate a sarcophagus of solid silver housing one Vseslav, Prince of the long-gone kingdom of Polotsk. Remove said remains and secure the vessel for transport."

She paused and looked back and forth between Anika and Francis.

"Am I," she said, signaling to Anika, "We... are we missing something here?"

"Well..." Jericho looked uncomfortable, and he knew it. *God damn it, Storm, why the fuck can't you take care of these types of things,* he thought. *The Scorpion already despises me, now let's just pile on more layers of contempt.*

"Well?" Anika was going to force some answers now as well.

The truck continued to navigate the long-abandoned byways of the land once known as the Principality of Polotsk. Situated in modern Belarus and landlocked by Lithuania, Latvia, and Russia, the ancient land was steeped in an abundance of myth and lore - none more widely known than that of the legend of the Baba Yaga.

She was the great and awful supreme witch - a sorceress trained in the forbidden black arts of the ancients, and a timeless, demonic presence that had haunted the dreams of the children of Europe and Asia for millennia.

"Jericho..." Serket leaned over and into the space between the front seats. "Jericho," she repeated. "We are here. We are with you until the end of whatever this is. Now show us the same respect and tell us what it is?"

Frank bowed his head and nodded.

"Fair enough," he said, then rose and gazed into her eyes. "Keeping you in the dark was part of my directive," he admitted. Screw Storm, he could bear some of this weight.

"Understood," Serket said, then retreated back to her seat and waited for him to entrust their mission's details to them.

"Naamah walks among us," he began, and paused.

Serket's face remained expressionless - all but her eyes, that is, which were alive with fire and fury. They were also alive with fear. Frank was sure of it.

"Continue..."

"Well, I don't know all the details - not much actually - of what is going on out there. I only know how it pertains to us and what we are doing in this God-forsaken corner of the world."

Alerik slowly turned to Jericho, who caught sight of the hulking Slav in his peripheral vision.

"No offense, man," Jericho quickly added, to which the driver grunted in disapproval.

"So," he continued. "We are to locate and enter the long-abandoned necropolis of Polotsk. It's a massive city cemetery of legend, adorned with mausoleums and funerary structures that rival those dreamt of by the likes of Lovecraft himself. Locate the final resting place of the Sorcerer Prince Vseslav Bryachislavich." Alerak spat symbolically at the mention of the evil ruler.

Jericho's eyes grew wide at the display. "Heard of him, I see?" he asked rhetorically, and laughed nervously. "Still feeling spite at the mention of his name, are we? Even after over a thousand years. Now that's how you hold a grudge." He laughed again nervously. No one else joined him.

"Please continue, for God's sake," Anika implored, a new pallor taking hold of her features.

"Of course," Jericho replied compassionately, noting her obvious growing terror. "Of course."

He cleared his throat, stealing a swig of water from the plastic bottle propped between his seat and the center console of the truck. The synthetic shell crinkled a miserable cacophony in the silence of the compartment, and he quickly wedged it back.

"Okay... sorry," he said, lifting his hands in mock surrender. "Where was I?"

"Naamah... Sorcerer Prince... Cemetery..." Serket said, leading him back in.

"Yes," he blurted out. "Sorcerer Prince. A sorcerer who apparently studied the ancient ways of the first people and devised a plan to trap and destroy the Baba Yaga. This plan was as much for his own glory as it was to protect his people. And as Storm so aptly pointed out, self-serving plans rarely achieve their desired result."

"Wise Alexander Storm," Serket mused.

"Yeah, well, he was dead-on here," Jericho continued. "He failed to destroy the Baba Yaga, and she first turned his city into a necropolis. That's why this is like no other burial grounds any of us have ever entered. A dark curse holds a perimeter around the lost town to this day. Then after the Yaga finished with the town, she turned her attentions to the prince, cursing him for all eternity to be a slave to the lunar beast, to walk as a wolf on the four cycles of the moon. Full, new and the half phases. Four times a lunar cycle, Vseslav would transform into a monstrous werewolf, ravaging and mutilating every living thing that crossed his path."

Jericho paused as the driver tapped him. "10 minute," he informed them in his broken English. Frank nodded in understanding and returned to the tale.

"So, after over one hundred years of this murderous cycle, the countrymen, landowners, and dignitaries had had enough. For although the prince was a super proponent for his people twenty-six or twenty-seven days a month, the other four days were too much. No matter how much good he did when he was dressed as a man, they couldn't look past the wolf. So, the elders devised a plan, and forged the massive silver casket."

"To imprison the prince?" Anika blurted out.

"Yup." Jericho shook his head. "And now, we're going to borrow the silver prison for an even greater evil."

"Naamah." It was Serket who offered the answer this time.

"Yup," Jericho said, nodding in sync with the Egyptian Magi, and a moment of silence ensued.

"Fucking Storm," Serket said, pushing the words through gritted teeth.

"Ha ha." Jericho perked up, his voice trembling. "Fucking Storm."

Serket closed her eyes and began to shake her head side to side. Soon, giddy bursts of what could only be characterized as laughter escaped her as well.

Anika, not to be left out, joined in the nervous banter, and for her part, softly piped up, "Fuckin' Storm."

Shocked, Serket and Jericho laughed even harder.

"Yeah... fuc'nin Stoorm," Alerak said, putting his two cents in. The three froze, silent, staring at one another and suddenly burst into full-on laughter at the driver's contribution.

"We here," he announced, slamming on the brakes.

"We here," Jericho said, spinning in his seat. "Of course we here!"

The laughter that followed was a wholehearted release of insurmountable tension. It was loud – loud enough to be heard from outside the confines of the car. Loud enough for the wild stags to take notice and take flight. Loud enough for the night owls to catch the din and spin their heads in the truck's direction. Loud enough to send the ground mice and foxes scattering.

And loud enough to reach the rotted, decaying ruins of the cemetery.

38

Balial repeated the words of the Copper Scroll as he approached the section of city wall he surmised it referred to.

"Beautiful dark one," he said, beckoning to Naamah. "Your prize lies beneath these foundation stones."

Slinking forward from the shade of the adjoining mud and stone wall, she smiled slyly at the jinn. *Beautiful dark one,* she repeated in her head. She simply adored the old ones. The jinn especially. None were more vicious and evil in both their appearance and actions, yet a conundrum prevailed in their manners and old-world manner of speaking and interacting. They were frozen in time. This trait was truly advantageous to her current plight. Even the archaic, hidden city they were in now could have been brand new three thousand years ago. The structures and landmarks that stood at the time of the drafting of the scroll remained as they were - a snapshot in time.

"Your assistance has been invaluable, cousin," Naamah purred as she moved past his hulking frame. Atticus had remained silent and still, tucked away in the background of wherever they passed since an incident at the first city when his human stench had launched a demonic stampede that would have led to him being flayed alive and left to rot out in the desert sun. If not for the commanding respect and authority worn by Balial, Atticus the Great would currently be Atticus the Late.

"Your quest is admirable, Naamah," Balial said, shaking a fist and spreading his massive wings. "For too long our kind has dwelled in the shadows, confined to the ruins of mankind. We are the superior race. We are the rulers of the skies and stars. We deserve our time. And you are taking steps to bring this to fruition, practically on your own." He shook his massive head in disgust at his brethren's current state of stagnation. "Make it so, beautiful dark one... I await your call to arms."

Climbing upon the ruins of a collapsed structure, he flapped his wings once and stirred the sand around him into an air-bound dance.

"And you," he bellowed out, pointing at Atticus. "You..."

Atticus felt his body begin to tremble once more.

"For your service to and for my queen, you shall always walk under the protection and watchful eye of Balial."

Atticus let the air trapped in his lungs burst forth and he gulped back some anew. Smiling, he lifted a hand in thanks.

Balial smiled and beat his wings into a fervor, lifting him high into the cloudless sky, so far and so fast that he was nothing more than a dark speck on the face of the blue sky in a matter of seconds. Atticus continued to look to the sky.

"Wow," Naamah called out to him. "Look who made a new friend."

39

"Just over that mountain ridge, Mr. Storm," the pilot spoke, the words entering their ears through the headphones they each wore. "I have two blips on the rad. That's got to be your targets. There is nothing else out here."

Alexander leaned forward and tapped the pilot on the shoulder. He turned and Alex offered him a thumbs up.

~

OVER THE RIDGE, blazing a trail through the hot desert sun, Naamah and Atticus walked side-by-side in silence. They had made quick work of the staircase wall and had no trouble exposing the antechamber within. There, lying unspoiled for a mini eternity, was the Book of Flesh. Naamah had scurried like a small animal into the hollow and retrieved the text.

She emerged from the hole with the book held squarely against her chest, arms crossed over the large volume, and there it had remained as they made their way back towards civilization.

"You okay, Atticus the Great?" she said, turning to check on him at her side.

"I will be fine after a hot shower, a roll in the sack, and a good meal," he said, laughing.

"In that order," Naamah said, playing with the mortal.

"Well, no," he started, and thought better of skipping the shower. "Actually, yeah, probably that order... I think you would prefer the shower first, at this point."

"The filth doesn't bother me, silly boy," she said, laughing. "You don't smell any different to me right now than you normally do."

"For real?" Atticus said, grimacing. "That really sucks."

"You know what else sucks?" She licked her lips and closed the distance between them. "Hot, sweaty, demon whores... of which I am one."

The conversation began to stir something in her, and she paused. "You know what," she whispered around his ear. "Why don't we just take care of number two on your list right now, right here."

A large grin spread across the man's face. *Fuck, yeah*, he thought, *never fucked in the open desert before.*

Naamah shifted the compendium to be cradled in one arm and slid the shoulder of her robe off, exposing one firm, perfectly formed breast to the unforgiving desert sun. She swapped her arm holding the book and looked up to find his linen pants around his ankles, his large member protruding skyward from his body. Atticus watched in anticipation as the second shoulder slid off her body, taking the entire robe with it to the desert sand.

Atticus whistled a standard catcall at the site of her exposed curves.

"You gonna set that thing down for a few?" he asked, pointing at the Book of Flesh.

"Not a chance," she said, laughing.

He laughed in turn. "Whatever... far from the weirdest shit you ever pulled."

Naamah was done speaking. She dropped hard, driving her bare knees into the hot sand. Leaning forward, she took him in her mouth. Her head bobbed and rotated as he moaned in sheer pleasure into the barren desert. Using her free hand, Naamah began to work her mouth and fingers in skillful unison, driving her sexual victim to the brink and pulling him back repeatedly.

Withdrawing her face from his body, she spun around and dropped forward, elbows into the sand. Lifting her ass high in the air and resting the side of her face in the sand, she commanded him.

"Fuck me," she growled, wiggling in the sun's rays with anticipation. "Fuck me now!" she demanded, and he complied. The raging sun and warm sand worked their union into a sweat-filled fervor, with the musky scents of their copulation swelling around them.

"Fuck me harder!" she squealed. "Make me cum!"

Atticus, lost in the ecstasy of their alliance, failed to notice the demon fiddling with the book, unlatching the ancient, weathered straps. He did not catch her opening the volume below her head. He was close now, and the outside world disappeared.

Atticus also failed to properly interpret the sounds emanating from Naamah's mouth, mistaking them for passionate moans in a demonic dialect.

"Atticus!" The word burst from her mouth like an explosion as she pulled away from his impaling and spun around to face her prey.

"What the hell?!"

The words barely made it past his lips before the demon shoved the open book out from her body at him. Immediately locked into a trance, Atticus stared into the open pages which were alive with secrets and revelation. He felt his strength drain first and could not move or drop. His mind reeled as the Book of Flesh wormed its way into his psyche, absorbing all his thoughts, all his memories - all that he was.

Naamah rose to her feet. She no longer held the book. It hung suspended in the air of its own accord.

The ancient text next went to work on his flesh and bone, and Naamah laughed exaltedly as she watched the deconstruction of Atticus the Great. She looked on as the book separated his being, cell by cell, molecule by molecule, and absorbed him into the pages.

Soon, there was nothing left but a pile of dirty clothes. The book slammed shut and dropped into the pillowy sand below. Naamah retrieved her robe and put it on. Bending over, she plucked the Book of Flesh from the grasp of the desert sand.

"I will miss you," she said to the pile of soiled clothes as she rummaged through them. "But only for a few minutes. I had to be sure the book's magic was intact."

Switching arms, she cradled the book and worked her free hand in the pants until she located what she was looking for.

"Gotcha!" she said, and smiled, lips pouting, as she rose with the leather pouch containing Solomon's Ring in it. Pulling the ring from the bag, she slid it over her slender finger. The ring, sensing the change in ownership, shrunk to a firm fit around Naamah's finger. Dropping the pouch to the sand, she resumed her march through the desert.

"One blip," the pilot said. "We have only one blip now."

Alexander rubbed his forehead and turned to the others.

“Prepare yourselves,” he instructed. “We will be dealing only with Naamah now.” He paused and rubbed his head once more. “And she has obtained whatever she went into the desert to find.”

40

Jericho's light was the first to find a structure in the darkness at the end of the overgrown path. He turned to Anika, who was right behind him, and waved his light in a circular pattern on the stone wall. Giving a few hand signals, she expressed her understanding. They were going to follow the wall until they found a way to get beyond it.

Serket had taken a path to the left when they had arrived at a fork about fifty yards behind them. She was a stealthy warrior, and Jericho did not pause to listen for her proximity. He would never hear anything - of that, he was fairly certain.

Jericho waved Anika on, and they moved slowly along the wall, eventually finding themselves at a crumbling mess of bricks and stones heaped in a pile where the continuation of the wall had once been.

Stepping over the debris, the pair entered a massive clearing. The moon was insanely bright now and illuminated everything around them - so much so, that they both doused their lights and allowed their eyes to adjust to the moonlight.

"My God," Anika let slip ever so softly. Her words were sufficient to catch a sideways glance from Jericho.

Sorry, she mouthed but emanated no sounds. He nodded and held out his arms as if to say, *my God,* and smiled at the girl, easing her tension a smidge.

Retrieving his cell phone from an inner pocket, Jericho snapped off a rapid-fire sequence of shots documenting the awe-inspiring size of the necropolis before him.

To either side of them were hundreds of tombstones of all sizes, shapes, and character designs - from angels and holy figures to creatures that resembled gargoyles and demons. Past the stone markers were stone and wood structures that went on for as far as the eye could see.

Anika leaned close to Jericho, and he bent down, bringing his ear to her mouth.

"You think it's buried? Do we need to dig?" she asked.

Frank shook his head and curled his expression as if to say *I don't think so.*

Anika smiled at him and nodded. She was happy to hear that. It would have taken months to dig up all these graves in search of a silver coffin.

SNAP!

Jericho's hand shot out to Anika's chest, halting all movement. Something had moved, and he was fairly sure it was not Serket. She would never approach unannounced from the front - that would be suicidal if they didn't recognize her. No, she was still off to their left. Something else had moved. Something large enough to snap a big branch under its weight. Peering hard ahead of them, Jericho noticed there was a cave-like entrance which had been cut into a mound or a hill of some kind. Tall structures jutted from the top of the hill and beyond, forming a mini city of stone.

Jericho pointed to the entrance and motioned for Anika to follow. Switching their lights back on as they approached the dark hole in the hill, they illuminated the opening.

There was not much to be seen at the entrance, and their vantage point offered no clues as to what lay beyond.

Shrugging, Jericho marched forward, passing the threshold into the cavernous hill. Still, he found himself unable to see beyond a few feet in front of him. *Must be an optical illusion of someone's making*, he assumed. Signaling for Anika to stay put, he took a few more steps forward until he found the cause of the obfuscation. There, Jericho found a wall cut at a ninety-degree angle. The intricate marvel of engineering stopped all light from entering or exiting from the interior.

Signaling for Anika to stay put once again, he followed the light-blocking wall to the end and stepped around to the interior of the dwelling. Jericho was awe-struck at what met him on the other side. Hundreds, no, maybe thousands of ignited candles adorned every possible nook and cranny of the walls. Their flames moved in unison, casting converging, and then diverging shadows about the whole structure.

Jericho stepped further into the clearing and was taken by surprise when he caught sight of movement directly ahead of him. Shinning his beam forward, he found its source. There at the center of the clearing, lying prone on her back and staring seductively back at him, was a woman. With hair as black as coal and eyes to match, she smiled and beckoned Jericho closer. Her ragged dress was hanging scantily from her limbs, one of her breasts were exposed, and her long, slender legs fidgeted in a slow dance on something metal below her. What was that below her? He moved his light around to get a better look. A scattering of linen and fabric lined the space below, and Jericho struggled to ascertain what the object was.

"Right size and length," he muttered to himself, flashing the light across the surface once more. He was sure he was catching glimmers

of metal. He would need to get closer if he was going to confirm his suspicions.

Moving forward at an even pace, he approached the alluring fiend. She was watching him, expressionless, and it made Jericho think of a spider sitting on the outskirts of its web, watching a moth flutter until it expressed all its energy and could move no more. A spider could then gingerly approach its dinner without fear of reprisal.

That was Jericho - the motherfucking moth in this scenario. There was no way in hell this bitch was real - lying about in her sexy ruined clothes waiting for the likes of him to wander into this desolate structure in this forbidden land. Yeah, right. Momma did not raise a fool. As nice as that thought was, this was clearly the devil's hand.

He took another step forward.

SNAP!

Spinning, he trained his light where he believed the sound of movement had come from. Nothing. Jericho made a mental note to himself that the circular shape of the stone structure was most likely wreaking havoc on the normal properties of acoustic theory. In other words, he really had no idea where that sound was coming from.

Returning his gaze, he was stunned to find that the woman on the coffin was gone. Tracing his light about, he searched his surrounding area for a sign of her movement. Nothing.

"Fuck it," he spat, and moved quickly to the platform the spectral beauty had been laid out on. Reaching it in mere seconds, he quickly stripped it of its adornments, exposing a splendidly ornate silver sarcophagus beneath.

Using his light, he walked around the coffin, investigating the sealed edge. Popping a spring blade from his belt and flicking it open, he jammed it in along the seal and began to drag it down the side. There was a series of popping sounds followed by an melliferous odor so powerful, it caused him to spasm and puke. Wiping his mouth on his sleeve, he reassured himself. "Nothing I could have done about that," he explained to the darkness. "Involuntary convulsion."

SNAP!

Jesus Christ. He had had it, and his nerves could take no more. "Where the hell are you? Let's get this happy horseshit over, huh?"

Silence followed, and he directed his attentions back to the metal cocoon in front of him.

"Jericho..." The yelling whispers, as he had coined them, came from the direction of the entrance.

"Anika," he spoke softly. Nothing.

"Now *I* have to do the damn yelling whisper, which I can't stand."

He moved to the other side of the coffin.

"ANIKA..."

SNAP!

That was behind him, and he spun around, shining his light into the dark crevices on the wall beyond the coffin. Silently he stood, watching... listening... nothing!

Eyeing the top of the silver coffin, he noticed some granules - some debris that had not been there a moment before. He stared at them inquisitively for a moment.

Then three things happened simultaneously. A barrage of rock and dirt hit and bounced off the top of the Werewolf Prince's coffin. Next, Anika stepped into the clearing and screamed....

"JERICHO! ABOVE YOU!"

And lastly, Jericho was struck on his head with such force that the ring of consciousness in his pupils filled and fluttered to blackout proportions.

"Stay!" He commanded Anika, and she froze. Rolling to one side of the coffin with practiced tactical maneuvers, he righted himself just in time to see the figure charge at him from the darkness. It was the sexy coffin woman - he was sure of that based on the tattered clothing. She had changed, though, and the festering crone of a beast that was headed at him right now held zero in common with the seductive witch that had been before him minutes earlier.

Grabbing several vials from his jacket, he tossed one, missing his target completely. She began to charge again. The Baba Yaga was real, and Frank Jericho was about to take the abomination on mano-e-mano, one-on-one.

Leaping to one side to avoid the charge, Jericho firmly slapped his hand down on the back of the beast's head as it passed. The holy water inside burst into the atmosphere with boiling fury, and a cacophony of shrill screams and wails filled the oval chamber.

Jericho patted down his pockets, trying to conduct an inventory of the weapons he had that he could use to defeat this demon. His pat down did not locate anything useful, and a slight pang of panic smacked him across the face. *How the fuck did I allow myself to be put in this position without the proper tools?* he thought. Reaching in his pocket, he withdrew his last vial of blessed aqua and spun in place, searching for the creature - waiting for the impending onslaught.

"FRANK!" Anika screamed, but it was too late. The Baba Yaga had Frank Jericho pinned to the stone floor, and Anika watched in horror as the demon witch lifted one hand high above its head. Like one of those time lapse videos you see all over the socials these days, plants growing, time passing, so did the nails on the Yaga's hand grow until they were at least six inches of unbreakable talons.

At the sight of the impending onslaught of razor-sharp talons,

Frank Jericho stopped struggling. He was not going out like that. No way.

"Come on, you fucking piece of filth," he growled up at the Baba Yaga, "I will have you on the other side – I will hunt you for eternity, you fuck."

The creature, clearly impressed by his fortitude, paused for but a second.

BOOM!

A deafeningly powerful blast blew the monster off Frank. He rolled to his right and sprang to his feet next to Anika. Looking at her hands, he realized Anika had no weapons - no shotgun.

"What the fuck?" he called out, and Anika shrugged.

"Yup." Serket sailed past them both like a wraith. "That's me."

"'What the fuck' is you?"

"It sounded cooler in my head," she called out from one of the shadows. "She's coming back, you know?"

Jericho tenderly shoved Anika deep into the shadowy cover of the entrance wall and dashed to the silver coffin.

The Yaga was still wailing from its wounds, but as both Jericho and Serket knew, she would quickly be healed. She was a black witch - a bride of the devil - and she had the ability to heal herself.

Jericho leaned on the silver coffin and righted his wobbly being. The silver was cold on his hands and arm.

"Hey," he yelled to the Egyptian Scorpion, "I have a brilliant idea!"

Serket dropped right in front of him as the demon's wails grew closer still.

"I think I have the same idea," she said, toying with him.

"What are the chances of that?" Jericho said, smiling. "You thinking like a pirate... "

"Right." Serket laughed nervously. She was almost on them now - the cries were so close, so angry. "And it's a horrible idea... nothing brilliant about it."

Frank paused. "Hmmm." He nodded his head. "Okay, maybe we *do* have the same idea."

The Baba Yaga was there now... returned to finish them all off.

Jericho and Serket had both moved to the far side of the silver coffin. In unison, they withdrew massive blades from somewhere on their person, and winding up for a powerful thrust, drove them into the seal of the coffin.

The creature froze.

"Climb, Anika!" yelled Jericho. "Can you scale that wall? Use the breaks and missing sections. Get off the ground!"

They could not see if she was complying, but Serket nodded to Jericho. "Good looking out, pirate."

"Fuck you, matey," he replied with a smile. "Break the seal!" he cried and transferred his aggression into the final thrust.

Like the top of a bottle of soda pop that had been shaken for a thousand years, the lid blew off and out into the chamber.

Jericho and Serket peered down into the interior of the coffin, their blood running cold in their veins. The massive werewolf inside struggled and snapped the inferior inner bindings that had been used to secure him for transfer to the coffin eons earlier.

Howling an earth-shattering roar, the wolf-man snapped up and out of its prison, traveling high into the still night air and coming down directly before his archenemy... the Baba Yaga.

"Really... REALLY... bad fucking idea, Francis," Serket cried out, retreating to the wall Anika had hopefully scaled. She was pleased to find her a good twenty feet up, and quickly joined in on the climb. From their vantage point, they were able to watch the two creatures of the night face off. The Yaga would slice talons of pain through the wolf, and in turn, he would bite chunks of putrefied flesh from her body. This went on for what seemed like an eternity, and the observers hoped it would be over before one or both demons caught sight of them. Jericho had not had time to make it to the wall and had simply crouched behind the silver casket. He let go an audible sigh of relief when suddenly the black witch perked up and darted to the exit into the necropolis - the exit opposite where Anika and Serket lay hidden, suspended to the wall like spiders.

The werewolf catapulted out into the night to chase down the witch who had cursed him for eternity. His muscles were fueled with hundreds of years of pent-up anger, hatred, and a blinding rage.

After waiting a bit for the monstrous duo's return, or perhaps just the victor, they decided the coast was clear.

"You all right, ladies?" Jericho asked as he approached the base of the wall.

"Bumps and bruises," Anika said softly, the ordeal amplifying her Egyptian accent.

"Let's get the hell out of here, please." Serket implored them to follow, and they did.

Activating a small, short range radio Alerak had given him, Frank pressed the button and spoke into the microphone. "The tomb is cleared... coffin is empty... send your men in and get it on its way to Mr. Storm."

"Rojjer."

The three giggled at his silly talk, once again.

"Are we mean?" Serket asked, halfheartedly. "Making fun of the poor guy."

"Nahh," Frank interjected. "Just letting off steam."

Reaching out, he touched Serket's hand. "By the way, nice shot. Thanks for the save."

She shrugged him off. "Hey, that's what we're here for, right? The save."

"Well, whatever the case me be... thanks."

"I wouldn't thank me yet," Serket said with a deep and hearty laugh.

"Why is that?"

"Because I intend to request that you help me clean up this little mess we just created after we are done with Storm's current mission."

"Sounds like fun," Jericho said, laughing out loud. "You can come too, Anika. I'll grab some milk bones and some raw steaks, and we'll make it a party."

The three friends continued to laugh as they walked to the truck. It would be the last time any of them laughed for some time to come.

41

The dull drone of a chopper spread across the barren desert like a rushing wind in a sandstorm. There was no protection from the sound in the open desolation of the sea of sand. The decibels found their way into every nook and cranny of the landscape, and could only be defeated by stronger, more intense sounds, which, based purely on their physical attributes, were louder.

Naamah, moving on a steadfast track towards civilization, heard the distant hum of the rotors. She had, in fact, no choice but to hear them. It was dead ahead, and judging by the intensifying level of sound, headed right for her.

Quickly surveying her surroundings, she spotted a cluster of stony hills about one hundred yards to her left. If she sprinted, she might be able to make it to the safety of their shelter before the incoming birds broke the horizon.

Wasting no more time contemplating her options, the demon was in an all-out sprint. Clutching her prized book under her arm, she worked the muscles in her legs until they screamed in agony. In less than a blink of an eye, she was at the petrified structure. Rough and pitted, the hills appeared very out of place. Having spent the better part of two days wandering an arid sandbox, she could not recall seeing any similar stones anywhere in the desert.

"Odd," she commented to the wind, running her free hand across the surface of the closest formation.

"What the..." She snapped her hand away. The rock was cold to the touch – freezing, in fact, and she lowered her body into the sand at its side to escape the view of the newly-arrived strangers.

"Fuck me," she whispered. They were here. How had they set down right on top of her? There was no way they were tracking her. The book had been walled up in a hidden jinn city for over a thousand years, and there was no way she was a host for any tracking devices. She was practically naked. The thin gauze robe literally left nothing to a lucky voyeur's imagination, and the boots had been with her since she plucked them, randomly, off a shop's shelf, having discarded her heels. She had simply walked out the front door of the store, and no one, save herself, had laid a hand on the clothes since.

Voices! She heard a discordance of barely articulated voices blending together with the dull, ever-present call of the choppers' rotors. She had to make a move. She could backtrack and find another route... but if they found her here, they would find her there.

"Who the fuck are these imbeciles," she questioned the entire scene. They had to be looking for her. Why else arrive here, now?

Leaning forward, she allowed the palm of her free hand to hit the sand and began to circumnavigate the rock cluster. Moving forward at a snail's pace so as to not alert the strangers, she happened to slip, and her shoulder launched forward, causing her to lose the support of her hand beneath her body. Tucking and rolling to limit both the noise level and the damage inflicted on her body resulted in the strangest thing - the exposure of a passage in and below the rock formation. She waived her hand in the void between the earth and the boulder. Further onward, the air felt cooler in the space below the rock.

Naamah shifted her body and lowered her butt onto the sand. Pivoting now, she swung her legs around until they hung suspended over the naturally camouflaged hole. Bending her knees, she prepared to slide into the unknown space, feet-first.

"NAAMAH!"

She froze in place. *What was this? Who was this?*

"Naamah." It was a man's voice, cold and serious. "Naamah, you are surrounded in all directions."

A tinge of panic crept across the demon's face.

"Naamah," he continued. "Surrender... step out into the light and submit to expulsion from this realm," the voice demanded.

Enough. She spat and rose to her feet. Moving slowly for the time being, she edged her way around her cover until she had an open view of these interlopers. These strangers who were invading the great empty desert needed to take heed now. These were the byways of her kin, the jinn, and if need be, she would summon them once more.

Naamah remained silent and still, focused on the space between the two choppers that had landed side by side. Every few seconds, she was able to catch sight of a figure pacing past the space her view afforded. There were several women in the group, although she had not recalled hearing their voices. The one challenging her, calling her name, calling her out - his voice rang a note of familiarity, but she couldn't place it. She needed to hear more.

Dust and pebbles suddenly rained down on her from above. Shielding her eyes with a cupped hand, she was able to make out a set of boots milling around above. This fucker really *did* have her surrounded.

"Naamah!"

It was him, above her. She saw him now, and recognition consumed her free thoughts.

STORM!

"Enough!" she cried, as Alexander dropped to a knee and peered cautiously into the opening below. And there she was, in all her glory, the ancient scourge, the seductress, the vile harlot... and she had nowhere to go. She was essentially surrounded, having boxed herself in a corner.

"Storm!" she screamed up to him. "Storm..." He knelt again to get a better view. "I have reached my limit with you, you fuck. Let me introduce you to Momma's little helper. Asmodeus!"

Stepping from the cover of the rock formation, Naamah thrust her fist in the air. Solomon's ring sparkled in the vicious sun, and it instantly began to glow and smoke.

"Ascend, oh wicked one," Naamah said, beckoning the demon to come forth. "Heed my command, oh great and powerful Asmodeus."

A section of space directly in front of the female demon began to ripple, and smoke emerged from a tear in the fabric of reality. The Prince of Hell suddenly became visible on the other side of the fissure in time. Punching a gloved fist through the two realms, the demon grasped the outer world as if it were a solid wall, and pulled himself through, emerging onto the desert floor.

"Destroy them!" Naamah screamed. "Destroy them all!"

Alexander had not planned for this. He had been caught off guard.

Dashing to Doc's side, he grabbed the pilot by the back of his neck and drove him towards the choppers.

"The girls," he commanded. "Get them from this place!"

Storm needed to say no more - Doc understood. He rounded them up together and drove them back into the chopper. Diving into the cockpit, he pulled the yolk and had the bird in the air.

"Where are you taking us?" Sam demanded.

"Shut up and strap in... now!" he commanded, and Samantha complied.

"I am getting to safety if you must know!" he screamed back, clearly agitated by the blonde's constant insubordination.

They watched from above as Alexander Storm withdrew a long blade and began an all-out assault on Asmodeus. The blows did not appear to inflict much damage, if any, but it kept the beast occupied long enough for the helicopter to make its escape.

"Doc!" Kate yelled.

He did not reply. Eyes forward, he was concentrating on flying the bird.

"Doc... Doc... Doc!" she cried in a near tirade.

"What?!" He spun around, fury in his eyes. "I am trying to fly us out of here!"

"Stop!" Kate fumbled with the clasp on her seatbelt. "Fuck... fuck," she bellowed in frustration.

"Wooo!" Samantha opened her eyes wide, shocked at her friend's vulgarity.

"Help me! God damn it, Sam."

Sam, who had been engaged in some over-exaggerated horseplay at Kate's expense, relinquished the charade show and popped her belt latch. Scurrying to Kate's side, she applied the same technique and had the belt open and over her friend's shoulders in seconds.

Pushing by Samantha, Kate hopped in the co-pilot seat.

"Strap in," Doc demanded.

"What?" Kate yelled over the rotors to no avail. Turning to her friends in the rear, she shrugged her shoulders violently. "What the hell did he say?"

Samantha swapped her gaze back and forth between the two of them and realized he was telling her to belt up or get the fuck back in her seat. Kate nodded at Samantha and secured the seatbelt.

"Now!" Kate was still screaming. "You better fucking listen to me!"

Shocked again, Samantha leaned forward and shouted at Doc, "Listen, she never, I mean *never* swears like that. So..."

"So," Doc finished, "I should probably listen, aye?"

"Yes sir," Samantha said, winking at him. "You're picking up on all this so quick... keep up the good work."

Doc shook his head in little shifts and cast Sam a crooked smirk. "You are quite odd, my dear."

Samantha flipped her long blonde locks to the side. "You ain't seen half of it," she toyed.

"Hey," Kate reached out and punched Doc square in the shoulder. "Are you two flipping kidding me?"

Kate's punch sent the chopper into a tizzy, but Doc quickly righted the aircraft - so quick, he was pretty sure no one even noticed that they all almost just died in a fiery chopper crash. Scanning his passengers' faces, they appeared unphased - all but Sam.

She was smiling at him when their eyes locked. "Nice moves, rockstar," she mouthed. Doc gave a slight bow.

"Man, I really miss Lobo right about now," Abigail sputtered out.

"What?" Sam yelled at her. "Why would you ever say something like that?"

Abi shook her head in an annoyed fashion and put a hand up.

Grabbing the co-pilot's headset from a hook in front of Kate, Doc secured the headphones on Kate's head. Giving her a thumbs up, he spoke, "I am all ears, Kate."

She nodded and started with a great deal of forced calm. "I've been texting with Keith," she said. Doc nodded his head.

"When the shit hit the fan, I dropped him a pin. Turns out they were like a mile away." She couldn't contain her excitement. "They're pulling up to Alexander's location now!" she yelled. "Turn this thing around... NOW!" she shouted into the mic.

Looking between his passengers, he realized it was not up for discussion, "Fuck it... when in Rome... or actually, when in the Dead Sea, right?"

"Right," said Sam with a smile.

"Riiiight," mimicked Abi, who received one of Samantha's signature snake bite pinches, to which she let out a yelp and viciously rubbed the fast-rising welt on her arm.

Doc landed the chopper and cut the engine to give way to unimpeded communication between what was becoming a very large group.

Niceties were paid instantaneously, and the parties moved on. All except for Kate and Keith - whose lips were still locked.

"Get a room, you idiots," Sam said, laughing. "You're making all us single folk feel uncomfortable."

"Where is Storm?" Abigail wore a look of dread on her face as she pressed Decker for answers.

Kate, relinquishing her grasp on Keith, turned to second the question. "I didn't even realize he wasn't here." She sounded instantly exasperated. "Where is he?"

Decker stepped forward and began to offer his best rendition of events. "When we pulled up, Storm was locked in hand-to-hand combat with a demon. Asmodeus, if I am not mistaken. Storm looked roughed up, but okay."

"Where is he now?" There was a higher degree of panic in Abigail's voice. "Did anyone see?"

"Hold it... hold it." Decker rubbed her shoulder. "Listen for a minute, will ya?"

Abigail nodded.

"So, all of a sudden, the demon freaked," Decker continued. "Became more concerned about what was just beyond his vision, what was at the perimeter maybe... I'm not really sure, but the demon disobeyed the ring bearer..."

"Naamah, by the way," Asar added.

"Yeah." William shook his head. "Naamah."

"Continue, please." Abigail pressed them on as if waiting for some tidbit of information, some minutia that would impart some secret knowledge on her.

"So," William picked up, "Solomon's demon disappeared. Like right before our eyes. Vanished! See ya next time." He paused and took a gulp of water from the bottle in his hand.

"Decker!" Kate, Abigail, and Samantha all seemed to yell at the man in unison.

"All right, all right." He waived his hand and bobbed his head, then continued. "So, Storm, who seemed unphased by the demon's sudden departure..."

"That means nothing," Kate interjected. "We all know what a poker face Storm has."

"Agreed," Decker said, nodding. "So, as we were piling out of the van and heading toward him, he saw Naamah, I mean, we all actually saw Naamah exit through an optical illusion in that stone heap over there." He finished his account, pointing at the boulders and debris.

"And Storm?" Samantha threw her hands up and shouted at the top of her lungs. "The fucking point of that entire conversation, William!" She stared at him, side eyed. "Are you okay?"

"He followed her into the passageway," Decker said, giving Sam a hard look. "I'm sorry, I thought that was pretty obvious."

"Why would that be obvious, William?" Samantha was getting even madder. He was doing what she liked to call "doubling down." He fucked up. He should take his lumps and not add to the situation by throwing assumptions and fictitious exchanges into the mix.

Kate threw her hands up and began to head towards the rock formation Decker was referring to.

"Wait," Keith called after her. "Hold your horses, Wonder Woman." Catching up to her, he reached out and grabbed her hand, halting her forward progress.

Kate turned and flashed him a pretty evil look of her own. Regardless of her anger, he did not release her hand.

"Wait, please Kate," he asked, rather than ordered. "There's something obviously highly suspect about that hill of rubble."

"We have to investigate it, Keith. We have to find Mr. Storm."

"I agree." He tried to get what he thought were some rational arguments into the discussion but was unsuccessful.

"No, Keith." Kate was now heading back to the rocks. "If it was one of us who had vanished, Storm would already be inside, risking his life for us."

"I get it." Keith looked like a hurt puppy.

"Let's go," Kate said, and turned to the others. "I'm not kidding. We'll enter in pairs, like the buddy system."

"It's not *like* the buddy system," Sam cracked to Abigail. "It *is* the damn buddy system." They both giggled, releasing some nervous tension.

"Enough!" Kate was really worked up. "We have to find Alexander Storm, damn it!"

"Consider him found..."

Storm smiled as he exited the obscured passageway and nodded at Kate. “Thank you for your invaluable concern. It makes me feel that much better to know you have my back when I am not present.”

“What the hell, Storm?” Decker pushed forward to get closer to Alex.

“We must hurry,” Alex said, his face grave. “We must stop Naamah.”

“Is she still in there?” William asked.

“No, she is gone.”

“How?”

“Bathin paid her a visit.”

“Portal?”

“Obviously, William.” Alex walked along, motivating everyone to pile in the van.

“Who’s coming in the chopper, Mr. Storm?” Doc asked, falling in beside him.

“No one here,” Alex said. “Take the bird and fly to Jericho and bring him and the ladies to meet us. I’ll have him drop you a pin with GPS identifiers. I will do the same when we all get to where we are going.”

“Which is?” Doc asked.

“India,” Alexander grimaced. “Headlong into the end of it all.”

42

Naamah and Bathin stood before the spectacular Shree Padmanabhaswamy Temple in Kerala, India. Located on the southwest coast, the massive, gilded temple shimmered in the rich, all-consuming morning rays of the sun.

"So," Naamah said, tugging her companion's arm playfully. "What do you think of my little plan? And..." she said, smiling deviously, "more importantly, will you join me?"

Bathin leaned in and inhaled a deep helping of Naamah's scent. "I am considering it," she said with a laugh. "Seriously considering it."

"I told you," Naamah said seductively. "Once you've had Naamah... there's no going back."

Bathin nodded in agreement. "Sounds about right."

"So?"

"So..."

Naamah, getting visibly annoyed, changed her tone, and possibly her approach. "I have come to believe that this temple is the single most important location on the planet. What lies beyond the maze of doors and gates belongs to our kind. It is cosmic in nature... it is eternal... and these pig-like mortals have been surrounded by the wonder and the magic for thousands of years and still cannot make heads or tails of it."

"Heads or what?" Bathin was struck by the phrase, and she laughed again.

"Tails. You have never heard these words spoken before?" Naamah's brow wrinkled.

"I do not get around as much as you, my dear." Her fiery locks were being swept up in the air like tufts of dust weed blown across the plains in soft, gentle, acrobatics. Naamah watched, mystically intrigued by the display.

"Can't I just come and go as I please, and make no formal declarations as to whether I will assist you - after I have made some inquiries of my own? Why the urgency and the commitment now?"

Naamah took a few steps - more like a pacing movement rather than a decisive direction of travel. She had not planned to take on any further partners, or assistants, slaves - whatever - after she dispatched Atticus the Great Whiney Cunt, and she certainly wasn't looking for anyone comparable to herself. She saw how well that had played out with Moloch. Bathin had always presented herself differently than others of their kind. She was an evil fuck, up there with the worst of them, but she seemed satisfied to just exist. Either way, since her recent visit with Saint Peter at the pearly gates had stripped much of her supernatural prowess, she liked the idea of having an entity around with a certain compendium of skill sets - and portal manifestation was way up top.

"I will remain here with you..." Bathin smiled, and as a sultry tale played across her mind's eye, she bit her lip momentarily, overplaying the part. The two demons remained locked in an imaginary embrace, ignoring the intolerant cries and curses of the locals who passed them on that fine afternoon.

"So," Bathin said, rubbing her hands together in a devious manner. "What's on the agenda?"

"So many things," Naamah toyed back. "If my plans come together, if every gear is oiled, and every trap's forethought is on point, we will be standing in Hell very shortly… and Hell will be here."

43

The tremendous human transporter vehicle barreled through the streets and byways of India. They had landed at Cochin International Airport, approximately fifty kilometers west of Kerala, India. The entire Dragon Storm, as Alexander had coined them, was present and accounted for. Naamah had gotten a full day's head start on them due to her apparent newly formed alliance with the portal-hopping demon, Bathin. Now as they raced towards a secret meeting with an ancient Indian group known only as The Nine, Alexander decided that now would be the best, and most likely, only time he would have to review everything with them.

"If I can have your attention for several minutes, we can review."

There had been many rounds of reunification and tales of recent travels and adventures. The group was abuzz with excitement and promise, it seemed. They were clueless. They could very well be racing towards the demise of each and every one of them, along with the ultimate decimation and destruction of mankind. Yet their spirits were high.

"What's that, Alexander?" Decker had caught Storm's little internalized snicker in response to his own thoughts.

"Nothing... nothing. I was just amusing myself with some fond memories."

"This is one of *those* missions, Alex?"

He looked at Decker and said nothing. He didn't have to.

"Come now." Alexander assembled his fellow passengers close together and joined them tightly in the center of the transport.

Raising his hands, he called for and received silence.

"Here we all find ourselves again," he began at the beginning, filling everyone in on what had been going on with the others, until he finally arrived at the present situation.

"We are heading to a brief meeting with an ancient clandestine group known simply as The Nine. They are mainly concerned with meeting Kate, Samantha, Anika, and Abigail. The rest of us have other tasks - other requirements."

Azrael, who had been fast asleep on the bench behind Asar the whole time, suddenly shot up in her seat.

"Where are we going?" she called out nervously.

"Padmanabhaswamy Temple," Alexander answered over the din. Rising from his seat, he walked over to the young girl.

"Have you heard of it?" he asked, standing above her.

The young girl shook her head in the affirmative.

"You have." He smiled at Asar. "Well, well."

Extending a hand to Azrael, Alexander continued. "I don't believe we have been formally introduced. I am Alexander Storm." Bowing his head slightly, he felt her tiny hand slip into his.

"I am Azrael," she said, smiling. "My friends call me Az."

"Well Az, it is a pleasure to make your acquaintance."

"Ditto..." she said in a cute, curt voice.

"All right." Alexander returned to the center of the group. "I have analyzed what we can expect to find once inside the temple."

"How are we getting in?" Jericho said, rising to his feet. "That temple is rumored to hold billions in treasure. I can't imagine we can just stroll in there."

"I was concerned about this originally as well, but after much thought, I have to assume Naamah will have already opened a path for us."

Jericho shook his head. "So, no contingency?"

Alexander let a small laugh escape his nostrils. "This entire thing is a contingency plan, Francis."

"Right," Jericho said. Smirking, he fell back into his seat. "So basically, go with the flow until you can't flow no more."

"Sounds about right, old friend. Sounds about right."

Alexander spent the next few minutes explaining the history of the Temple. An exact date of construction was difficult to ascribe, but through historical literature, scholars were able to prove the structure had existed for many hundreds of years, if not over a thousand. Alexander then ran through the basics so that all the team would have a good working knowledge of the Temple. Dedicated to the god, Vishnu in the Anantha Shayanam Posture, the above ground aspects of the holy structure were elaborate and elegant, exemplifying the rich adoration of the gods.

It was, however, what lay below ground that was the basis for all that was occurring. In the subterranean passages of Padman, as Storm began to refer to it, lay six massive vaults. The size and expanse of these vaults were claimed in ancient historical texts to be unfathomable, and the mere fact that the vaults extended way beyond the confines of the structure above was common knowledge to all. Alexander answered as many questions as he could, having researched the location extensively through the years. Of the six vaults, five had been opened, their riches inventoried, and their shadow sides explored.

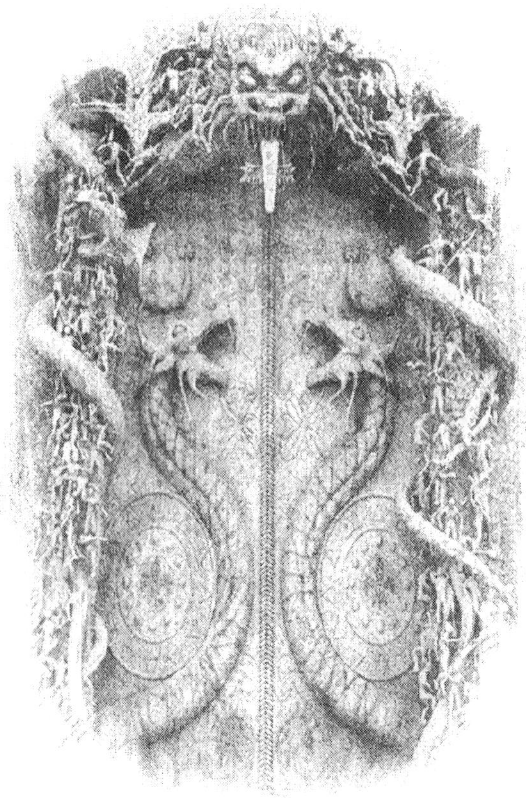

The one chamber that had not undergone this reveal was known as Vault B. Vault B was sealed by massive wood, steel, and stone doors. Above the entryway was the head of a massive malevolent demon, and at the doors' sides lay the guardians - serpent statues known as Naga. There was no record of the doors having been sealed, nor any records of them ever being opened. However, a recent accounting from one hundred years earlier spoke of the government forcing Vault B open. A team was sent to the massive doors to break the seal and inventory what was enclosed. They worked the doors for several days, to no avail, and they finally gave up when the workers claimed they could hear the sounds of crashing ocean waves right on the other side of the threshold. Work ceased, and they fled.

Alex had taken several questions and passed around several photographs before continuing once more. "The doors are rumored to have been sealed magically by the use of a secret chant for a period of time. A holy man - a Magi for example - could learn the mystical chants and open the doors by their voice alone. A cosmic locksmith, if you will, must be righteous as well - a warrior for God."

"Well, that should exclude our counters, no?" Asar reasonably concluded.

"That, my friend, is the general rule of thumb." Alexander began to withdraw papers and large texts from a bag on the floor. "And this is where the sacred book, the Book of Flesh - King Solomon's book of magic - comes in to play. Legend holds that if you open the book at its center and set it upon the floor in front of a lock such as this, the book itself will do all the work. I do not know exactly what that means, literally or figuratively, but it is what Naamah is depending on to be successful here."

"Wait." Sam looked as though she had just joined the party, oblivious to some of the previous discussion, but taking heed in the current line of discourse. "That bitch has this book, Solomon's magic book?"

"Yes, I believe so," Alexander stated with dismay. "She was carrying an ancient text when we crossed paths at the Dead Sea, so yes, I would say she does have the text she needs to proceed."

"And she has his magic ring, as well," Kate added.

"Correct, Kate." Alexander withdrew some sketches. "I believe the two items work in conjunction. She needs the ring to set the chant going to unlock the door."

Decker rose to his feet, starting to pace and worry. Anika reached out and held him in place, steadying him. "Naamah is not interested in gold or riches, so big picture, Storm... what the hell is down there?"

"Yes," Storm dryly replied. "Exactly."

"Huh?" Abigail had been following until hearing this.

"Hell, my dear girl. The whole elaborate creation... is to hold back Hell."

Members of the group fidgeted and exhaled copiously as madness played out in his words.

"My extensive research points to three more doors beyond the main. The first of these doors is a direct threshold to Hell. Not a passage to Hell, but Hell itself. The next is a shrine or tomb for a dormant cosmic entity - an entity of cosmic evil and an all-consuming and devouring darkness - and this darkness's name is Lilith." Expressions morphed and Decker cried out in dismay.

"The third of the doors I have been unable to classify. It may lead to one very exact location, or it may be a programmable doorway. I have not been able to ever gather one single shred of evidence or information regarding the third door."

Alexander rose to his feet, moving amongst his crew. "Please, please... we haven't much time. We are almost there."

Everyone settled down and allowed him to continue. "I believe this three-door system was devised so that at a prescribed point in time, Lilith would depart her realm, walk through the door of Hell, gather her loyal army, and then lead them out that door and through the third to some unknown location."

"Okay, so that's Lilith deal," Samantha said.

"My thought exactly," Abigail said, shaking her head. "Right... what does Naamah want from this?"

"Yeah, what makes that bitch tick?" asked Samantha. "What's she going to gain? Be the teacher's pet? That doesn't sound like her, does it?"

"Yes, well..." Alexander began to gather his things. "Excellent questions, ladies. I cannot answer them, nor are they necessarily relevant, but excellent, all the same."

"We're here," Doc announced as the vehicle slowed.

"Hey," Abigail said, moving in close. "Did Storm just diss us? Was that what an intellectual's jab feels like?"

Samantha made a ponderous face, as though wrestling with the notion. Without warning, she reached out and poked Abi in the belly.

"Hey!"

"*That's* what an intellectual's jab feels like." Sam laughed a real laugh, which was good, since it helped mask her real tears.

44

"Nothing comes through this stairwell," Naamah ordered Asmodeus, who nodded in compliance and understanding.

"Now *that* is a piece of jewelry a gal could really get used to," Bathin said with a laugh.

"Oh, yes." Naamah lifted the ring to her lips and kissed it. "Honestly, dearie, it's to die for."

The pair strutted ahead, leaving the ancient Prince of Hell at the only entrance into the cellars. Nothing would pass, although Naamah was not too concerned, as every living, breathing creature that had been in the temple when they arrived... was now dead.

Moving through the winding halls of the cellar, they found themselves at the end of the lit area of the southernly-branching tunnel. Bathin retrieved one of the lit torches from the wall and they proceeded further in. As they reached the end of what must have easily been a mile of tunnel run, they stepped into a relatively large antechamber. There, before them was the stuff of nightmare legend - the great door of Vault B, with an extruded demon head above, and stone Nagas to the left and right.

Naamah approached the door, laid her hand upon it, and pressed her ear tightly to it.

"I'm coming," she whispered to the dust laden wood of the door. "I'm coming now."

Removing herself to the center of the room, she began to empty the satchel she brought. She placed the linen-wrapped book down upon the damp, mold ridden dirt, but did not unwrap it.

"First," she said aloud, "let us ready another line of defense."

"Expecting company?" Bathin asked, more in jest.

"Oh..." Naamah looked up with a serious tenor in her eyes. "Most definitely."

There was a quiet pause as Naamah set to work arranging the necessary protocols - lighting candles and such. When she finished, she returned to the magic text and unwrapped it, placing the linen wrap on the floor first, then the book.

"Is there anything I can do to assist? Lend a hand?"

"Actually," Naamah said, grinning devilishly, "there is... strip your body bare."

Bathin laughed at her playfulness until she realized she was making a necessary request. "Of course," she said, loosening her skirt. Naamah watched as it dropped into the filth of the ancient cellar. Bathin lift her legs with slow, deliberate movements and stepped out of the ring of fabric at her feet. She wore nothing under the skirt, and her body glistened and flickered in the torchlight. Next, with one smooth move she lifted and removed her blouse, and once again there was nothing below. Her breasts bounced with her movements, and her large nipples were fully erect in the cool air.

"How's that?" she teased. "Does it receive your approval?"

Naamah said nothing, her smile and expression speaking without words. She winked at her companion. "Something to look forward to later, perhaps." Then she returned her attentions to the task at hand.

45

Doc had followed Alexander's directions to a "T," parking where he had instructed while facing the direction required. It had ended up being no easy task for the gigantic vehicle, and now he waited. The current address had been their first stop. He watched now as the main door flew open and four female warriors emerged, dressed in the old way, bearing weapons from another time. Their faces, which were marked and painted with black tribal war paint, were stoic, and they entered and sat in the vehicle without saying a word.

SECONDS LATER, he saw Azrael approaching the vehicle and opened the door for her.

"Hello, Doc," she said, smiling. He raised his hand in a high-five, which she hit as she climbed in. Doc returned to the driver's seat, and they were gone - set on a straight course to Padmanabhaswamy Temple to join the others.

Doc adjusted his rearview mirror and inspected each of them.

"Looking good, ladies," he said with a smile. "Looking really good."

A short time earlier that evening, Kate, Abigail, Samantha, and Anika had entered a large home at the dark end of the finished portion of a cul-de-sac. Anika had carried a large duffle with her, and she led the girls through the door and into the darkness beyond. Moments later, Samantha had returned to their vehicle.

"They say the child must come as well," Samantha relayed to Doc, who gave the message to Alexander, who appeared to be in thought for a split-second before nodding his head in understanding.

"Azrael," he spoke softly, turning to face the child. "Be a dear and accompany Samantha and the other girls, please? Thank you." He ushered Azrael to the exit.

As Asar rose from his seat and began to follow her, Alexander stepped between them as the girl passed.

"And where are we going, my jolly Egyptian brother?"

"With the girl," Asar said, pointing ahead at Azrael, who was exiting the vehicle. "She is my ward, for now."

"And maybe forever, Asar, but she is in good hands, and you are needed here."

The vehicle's doors locked, and Doc readied for departure once he received word.

"Asar," Alex called out, as his friend began returning to his seat. "Might I have a word?"

"Of course." Alex knew he was furious over the separation, but he would always act the gentleman. "What is it?"

Alexander put his arm, as best as he could anyway, over the large man's shoulders and brought him in close. "You do realize that the girl is a phantasm, don't you?"

"What?" He could not contain the level of his voice.

"It is true, my friend. She is not among the living. I am surprised you could not see that. We must be cautious around her."

"That is pure nonsense," Asar continued.

"William, please join us."

Decker walked over and dropped in the seat next to Asar. "What's up?"

"I was just explaining to our friend here that Azrael is not like other little girls. Can you give us your insight?"

"She's something, isn't she," William started. "I'm just not sure what."

Now Asar looked ashamed. "Forgive me, Alexander," he said, lowering his head. "I did not sense it."

"Rubbish, Asar, don't act the fool. She obviously was meant to be here - with us."

"I don't follow, sir." Asar glanced at Decker for any direction.

"The Nine just summoned her into their preparation," Decker said, taking a deep breath, "I've got to assume she's part of a preordained course of action. Who knows Asar," he said, laughing, "she may end up saving the world."

"Or at the very least, saving our hides," Alexander said, smiling at them both. They were all in a good place mentally. The battle to come would ensue with his people at their prime, their maximum - as though a steel band were woven through their connection to one another.

It was a good night to go to war.

~

~

EPILOGUE

"What of Egypt my friend?" Alexander had stolen away to the corner of the dimly lit road. His eyes seemed to be darting in all directions and it made Frank a little uneasy.

"Egypt was very fruitful Alexander."

Jericho considered whether he should get into the details of the trap he almost didn't escape, and how a little background and insight would have gone a long way, but thought better of it.

"I found what you were looking for. It was an amazing setup and I honestly can't believe it stood the test of time."

Alexander nodded, "Thank you Jericho," he smiled. "I can always count on you when it is most urgent."

Frank smiled. He couldn't help himself. Knowing something and hearing it were two very different things.

"Do you have it with you?"

"Of course," Jericho scrunched his forehead, "never left my possession."

"Excellent," Alexander began to move from the shadows, "deliver it to Doc who has been apprised. He will secure the items until we are finished here."

The two proceeded to join the others when Jericho tugged Storm to a stop.

"Did a little research," he whispered now, "this have anything to do with resurrection?"

There was a long pause, and the others began to call after them. Alexander turned and began on his way again.

"Some questions, Francis," he spoke over his shoulder, "are better left unanswered."

~

~

ABOUT THE AUTHOR

Anthony DiPaolo is an author from New York whose own literary interests lie in the classic realms of Lovecraft and Poe, and the modern works of Preston & Child and Stephen King. A deep passion for Egyptology and archaeology, as well as the tales and legends that surround ancient cultures, led to the basis of his current series: The Dragon Storm.

Writing in the sphere of what some have termed "Archaeo-Horror" - Anthony melds together the real life locations and legends of the ancient world and his own brand of supernatural plot twists and turns - to bring us fast paced, cliffhanger chapters and a cast of enigmatic characters in his supernatural adventures.

Anthony lives on Long Island with his wife, Michelle, and two sons, Anthony and Thomas, and their dogs, Sam and Frodo.

ABRACADABRA is the second book in The Dragon Storm series, and is a cliffhanger, two-part adventure. Watch for the second half coming soon.

Visit The Dragon Storm Web
www.DragonStormNovel.com

ALSO BY ANTHONY DIPAOLO

The Dragon Storm: GATES

Made in the USA
Middletown, DE
06 November 2023